SORTING THE APPLES & PEARS

Charlie —

Best wishes

Books by Peter Hayden:

The Adventures of Stringy Simon series, vol. 1 - 6

The Headmaster's Daughter

The Day Trip

And Smith Must Score...

Sorting the Apples & Pears

The Poppy Factory Takeover

(Details and order form at the back.)

Crazy Horse Press
53 Stourport Road
BEWDLEY
DY12 1BH
[+44 (0)1299 403201]
phayden@crazyhorsepress.com
www.crazyhorsepress.com

ISBN 1 871870 26 7

Printed by T. Snape & Co Ltd. Boltons Court, Preston PR1 3TY [01772 254553]

THANKS TO SCHOOLS

Much of what appears in this book was originally written in schools, during writing workshops. I had no idea it would become useful, just wrote whatever I could when the workshops were underway. I usually leave schools with a copy of what I have done, but have only started putting the name of the school on the page in the last year or two, which means I can't remember where I was when I wrote many of the pieces.

So... if you recognise a passage in this book as something I wrote in your school please get in touch, it would be lovely to hear from you, and I will acknowledge it in the reprint. These are the ones I did record:

Mr Benson's music lesson, and mum working at the Texaco garage were written at Sandcross School, Reigate.

Karen's mum snogging with Graham was written at Silloth Primary School, Cumbria, sitting by an old churchey window that looked out over the Dumfries coast.

The discussion about a holiday in Spain was written at Ducklington Primary School near Oxford.

The section with the light dimmer hanging out of the wall and Karen fixing the tap, was written at Willesborough Junior School, near Ashford, Kent.

The passage where Miss MacAlister is suspended, and a piece about Miss Stanislaus (I called her Miss Delaney at first), were written at St Mary's C.E. Primary School, Southampton, just across from the football ground - but it didn't put me off.

The whole section about the author was written at a brilliant all-day workshop in Solent Junior School, Southampton.

Heidi getting loads of house-points (they have become stars in the book), was written at Alexandra County Middle School, Northumberland.

The section about Heidi's dad and the Needles was done at Medina Primary School in Portsmouth.

The wedding section was fun to write because I kept taking it to different schools and continuing it. It started off at New Seaham Primary School in Co. Durham, carried on at Cullercoats Primary, North Shields, and finished at Dorridge Juniors in Solihull, near Birmingham.

Shaun's potion for the new baby was written at one of my favourite schools, Selsdon Primary near Croydon, which I have visited five times.

The passage about Corrie's hen-night was written at Morpeth Road County First School in Northumberland.

The holiday in Gran Canaria was written in another school I visit regularly, Sir Harry Smith Community College near Peterborough.

Thanks to everybody in all those schools, plus the other ones that I hope to hear from when they see this.

Characters:

Karen Taylor -	aged 12, medium height, mid-brown hair, a good runner; her mum who works at the railway station and new boyfriend Graham; her dad, a salesman and VW Beetle maniac, and his girlfriend Carol; and young brother Shaun.
Kim Taylor -	cousin and best friend of Karen: same age, average-looking, fair hair, blue eyes, some freckles, bigger than average nose, a good runner and keen horse-rider; her mum, (Karen's Aunt Rache); her weird dad (Karen's Uncle Don), and crazy little brother Ryan. Kim's older sister is Corrie, who gets married to Dave.
Gramps -	Karen and Kim's grandad Melvin – was married to Grannie Annie, his second wife, and worked in the brewery till he retired a few years before this story starts.
Heidi -	has transferred from private school and joins Kim and Karen's class.
The Teachers -	MacAlie, tight face, small mouth, glasses, wears badly-fitting clothes; Miss Stanislaus, from a Mediterranean background, young, olive skin, shiny dark curly hair to her shoulders, wears modern clothes and jewellery.

The Caretaker - Hargreaves, short and energetic, clatters around with a ladder all the time, and Sophie his mad dog - she is ninety-seven dog years and has a huge pink belly with nipples all the way down.

The Author - 50-ish, very scruffy; his dog is a Collie cross-type, also scruffy.

“Man muss noch Chaos in sich haben,
um einen tanzenden Stern gebaren zu konnen.”

[you need a bit of chaos inside yourself
to give birth to a dancing star]

Nietzsche

For Carrie

Introducing...
A Year in the Life of Karen Taylor

Year 6, last year of juniors. The year when the child-part of your life ends and the adult-part begins. Supposedly. The most strange, horrible, wonderful year of my life so far.
If I could have just taken a picture of it I would have, but you can't can you.

But.. there is something - my diary - which I'm going to chuck soon, most of it's fairly boring and crappy anyway, but not before I've taken out the major bits and put them together properly. So here goes...

Don't know what genre it is - comedy, tragedy...
bit of both.

Thurs 4th Sept

There's a bloke peering at me from behind the blue-speckled goggles and a gas-mask thing like a fly's nose. He's a Beetle collector. Nope - wrong, he's not an anorak going round old piles of wood and compost with a small net and jam-jar, he's a Volkswagen Beetle collector.

He's not peering at me this very minute, that's how I'm picturing him in my imagination. He buys old wrecks and does them up and flogs them, that's why he wears the mask, stops you inhaling paint. There's still one in the garage now, not exactly a whole one, he hasn't found anywhere for it yet. It's like the last bit of him still with us, just hanging in there not quite letting go. The engine's poking out of the back like entrails, it's meant to be like that, Beetle freaks think it's cool. All it needs now is a front wing and passenger door. Then he'll drive it away I suppose, and that will be that. People pay good money for old Beetles, they're collectors' items.

Underneath the paint-mask I would say dad was about average-looking for a middle-aged parental. He's thirty-four, quite short, short hair, round smiley face - bit like a monkey when he gets silly but otherwise he's ordinary enough not to embarrass you at parent nights and stuff.

The walls of the garage are brilliant - like rainbows where he sprayed all the different colours. We were allowed to graffiti anywhere in the garage, as messy as we liked, cause the next time he sprayed a car he just swished it over the wall to test it, and there's the last lot of graffiti covered and a nice clean space for the next lot.

* * *

Dad is a salesman. His region is the South-West and the Midlands, which means he has to go to firms right down in Cornwall, across as far as Peterborough and up to Stoke. I've been with him, one half-term when mum was ill and Shaun was only two. It was the most boring half-term I ever had, I would rather have stayed in and done a project. The firms dad goes to are all on industrial estates, which look the same anywhere - they're slapped down the cheapest way possible on a few acres of tarmac just outside of whatever town it is. The access roads are always unmade, they have rubble and mud and pot-holes with puddles, the car rocks around on its suspension when we get to a place, that's how I know we're close.

The firms are always in cheap-built ugly square blocks, basically a factory or warehouse with a brick extension tacked on, and this is the part where dad usually does his business.

He sells office stationery - all sorts of office equipment from staples and elastic bands right up to photo-copiers and computers.

When I was little I had anything I wanted to do with offices - coloured gummed squares which I used to stick into shapes, like square chickens, square rabbits, etcetera, felt marker pens, coloured staples which I could clip together and wear as a necklace - anything.

But now I'm just bored with that kind of stuff, and the thought of dad making me go in and out of tiny brick offices with one little fan-heater and a dying spider-plant while he drinks coffee out of a polystyrene beaker makes me feel sick.

* * *

I once tried to get him on Millionaire. It was after you-know-what, him moving out. He'd popped in to pick up a few things. I was possibly trying too hard:

'Come on dad, you can do it, you always know... It's not scary, just a camera, you're not scared of cameras are you? You are? Oh, what bit are you scared of - their massive jaws? Fang teeth? Their huge poisonous sting? Well - don't be so pathetic, just have a go. It doesn't matter if you do lose, people won't think any worse of you... Who will? What d'you mean lots? What lots? Mum wouldn't - would you mum? There, see? She says not. Only a little bit. You wouldn't look stupid... Alright, but not to me, I'd be proud of you, go on dad, please...'

* * *

Still 4th of Sept

Mum used to work at a petrol station on the Mansfield Road. She was called the manageress, but as she was the only one there half the time, it just meant she had to check everything on the shelves, get the till-roll right at the beginning and end of the day, open up and close. It was an easy job - most people are in a hurry at garages and just want to pay - but very tiring. Some weeks she got up at four-thirty in the morning and some weeks she started later but had to work till after midnight.

Her shifts were so unsociable that she and dad hardly saw each other, they would finish a shift at work and have to start a shift with us. That's when dad started playing around...

Mum is one of those people who has written to an agony page - in fact, she wrote to loads, because she couldn't think of anything else to do. She still loved dad, but she knew she had to make a stand. One paper said ditch him, one said stay and give up your job, one said go to counselling. She took all the first advice, from the Daily Mail, to kick him out, and a bit from House and Home which said change your job. She's been working at the rail-station ever since, it's better hours and they get uniforms.

It was in the garage one Christmas where it happened - she told dad to go and not come back - which is not a bad place if you think about it. I mean, real Christmas started in a stable didn't it? So I reckon it's right that ours started in the garage, where he did the cars.

That was a bad year, the year he left. The first part of it was mum crying all the time and dad occasionally coming and taking me and Shaun out. It always caused a row, then dad would do really extravagant things to try and cheer us up, which wasn't what we wanted.

Then one time he brought his new lady along. Didn't bother us, it was quite nice really, we didn't know who she was but at least she got him laughing. But then mum found out and refused to let him take us out for months afterwards. That was when I really knew.

* * *

{By the way, mum doesn't know it yet, but she's pregnant. Not by dad.}

*   *   *

I suppose I'd better introduce myself being as I am the main character, not being big-headed or anything.

Well, I'm Karen, Kaz to my mates, Shaun's sis and substitute mum and sometimes substitute dad - but that's not really me that's who I am to him. I'm... er, medium height, medium brown hair, quite a good runner, I've been in the county championships...

God this is embarrassing. I'll do it as if I'm Kim, describing me...

'Well, Kaz is quite funny sometimes, she sticks up for me, she's loyal, she would never say things behind my back...' (oops, better delete some of the stuff I've done about her) *'She listens to my problems. She's average-looking, not ugly but not Nicole Kidman..'*

Kim would have to say that, she's my best friend and cousin - two reasons she can't dish dirt... I don't really know if I am or not, average-looking. Some of the boys muck about with us and flirt, though it's not flirting really, anyway it's probably Kim they fancy.

My worst thing is I worry about other people all the time. In Canaria dad offered Shaun some money for the football table and he huffed off in a sulk, so I threw dad a comforting glance as if to say, 'It's alright, he doesn't mean it', then followed Shaun and tried to comfort him as well. I hate myself for that - they only shove me off the minute they don't need me anyway.

One of these days I'm going to just turn round and tell Shaun to grow up and get a life I swear it, and dad, and mum, all of them. Then maybe I'll be able to describe myself myself.

*   *   *

Tues 16th September

'Kim, before your 'rents split... did your mum, like - still kiss your dad much?'

'Course, every day. Twice actually. When he went to work and when he came back.'

'No, properly. I mean, snog?'

'Leave off, they're ancient.'

'I know... Only...'

'You've put me off my crisps now, yugh, prawn cocktail. What's wrong?'

'Well - our mums are about the same age, right?'

'Three years different, bit less. So?'

'Well we were watching tele at the weekend and mum and him - her *bo* - just started. Right in front of us. It was horrible, proper snogging with noises.'

'God, poor you.'

'It's scary Kim. First dad had a new girlfriend, now mum has. Boyfriend. Graham. He works at the station with her.'

'Is he gonna be..'

'Step-dad? Dunno, don't think so, she's only just met him, I think. Well... I never knew he existed anyway, till the other day...'

'You can't be sure, adults work fast when they get going. No time left that's why.'

'That's what's worrying me. They snog like that if they're keen, don't they?'

'Old people, yeah. Corrie doesn't, she snogs anyone. Well, before Dave she did.'

'That's different though... I've got a feeling they might be in love.'

'Are you bothered?'

'Bit, yeh. He'll never be like dad. Says, "Call me Graham," like we're friends. Dream on. The Thin Controller, that's what I'll call him if he doesn't go quick. God, imagine him swimming with us like we used to with dad, he's so skinny if he went over the lane line he'd disappear for a couple of seconds.'

'Ha, Thin Controller - Thomas the Tank... '

'Tommy Tanker, yeh, that's him... She can't be serious. I'd move out.'

'You could always come and live with us.'

'Thanks Kim.'

How could mum ever swap him for dad? I mean, HOW? The Thin Controller for dad: I just want to cry I really do. And dad's just as bad with his bimbo, 'silly little tart' I think was mum's phrase not for our ears on one occasion, which is about right. Why do 'rents do that? If you're going to wreck the family at least do it for someone half-decent, please...

They're planning to take us on holiday for half-term, mum and Graham, cause everything was up the spout in summer with the divorcing stuff. Spain.

'Urgh, we hate Spain, too hot,' Shaun said, pretty good for a year three who's never been there. 'You said Florida this year, you promised.'

‘Dad promised,’ mum said, ‘and he’s not here anymore.’

‘No - cause of you,’ he muttered, just loud enough, and bolted for his room where he sat breathless on the Beckham duvet for ten minutes marvelling at his own daring.

‘It was dad who went, not me,’ she snapped. I hadn’t said anything. ‘And Graham knows a little place off the beaten track. I’m sure we’ll like it if we just give it a chance.’

You mean if we give Graham a chance... but while I was thinking it my mealy mouth said, ‘How far off the beaten track?’

Graham answered, cause it was his place. ‘Bout ten miles from Tossa.’

‘Ten miles where?’

‘Inland.’

‘So how do we get to the discos?’

‘Don’t be ungrateful Karen. Think about someone else as well as yourself for a change. Graham’s made an effort to include himself in the family, he didn’t have to, you’re not his children...’

Yes, but he’s working on it, the creep.

* * *

Friday 19th September.

Phone-call. Dad. Want to come away with me and Carol for a week. Half-term - Gran Canaria, nice and warm, you’ll have your own room. Don’t have to decide now, talk it over with mum, give us a ring back.

I wander down the landing to Shaun.

'C'n I come in?'

'You already are.'

'Alright alright, keep your kegs on.' I've got a bit of a sparkle in my eye... 'Canaries. Dad says he'll take us. What d'you reckon then?'

'What about mum though, she's booked Spain hasn't she?'

'She could always cancel. Anyway, she might like it - bit of freedom... What shall I say? Shall I ring back and say yes?'

'Not sure...'

'Come on, let's, we don't have to suck up to Carol. At least we won't be stuck up a track ten miles from Tosser.'

I say it like that to make him laugh.

'...And when we come back it will be fireworks then Christmas.'

'O.K. then. You ring...'

We talk to mum, she's fine. Fine about lending us to *her*. She knows we won't swap sides.

And she's right. Carol, dad's bimbo, actually has a bit of a problem if you ask me. She's scared of growing up. You can say how does a person aged twenty-seven get to be still scared of growing up? Twenty-seven, it's disgusting, I feel so embarrassed for dad, making an idiot of himself. But she is scared - there's something about her, she's kind of dipsy, she thinks like a girl, like she flirts with him like you do with your teachers when you first realise you can. Like Kim does anyway. It's not real, it's not adult. She's not adult - she's got a high girly voice and she still tries to dress young. It's O.K., she can get away with it, but why would she want to. At her age I would be wanting to show I was a fully mature woman (if I was one I mean), not the other way round. And the way she talks to us, like we're the same age, like she's trying to be one of us, one of dad's kids, the oldest. The favourite. That's it... she talks to him like he's her dad not her lover (urgh, pass me a bowl, I think my pepperoni topping's coming back up). When she wants something she flirts and sucks up to him, and if she doesn't get it she sulks.

I've never asked her but I can tell she's scared witless of having children of her own. That's one reason - why dad I mean - because he's already got a family nearly grown up (ahem, well, certainly in my case), so she can skip right over the sicky, getty-up-in-the-nighty, milky-breasty, measley, dirty-nappyey phase, the phase that makes a woman of you, and pretend we're hers.

Well, Caz - you can take us to the Canaries and pretend, but I've got news for you. I reckon he's going to get bored with you, and I reckon it won't be long before he does. Just an opinion, nothing personal: I reckon you're for the chop before the year's out. That's what my money's on. And then we get him back. Hopefully.

Kaz, Caz. It was in a magazine that dads marry mum-substitutes then get the feeling of old-age creeping up and have affairs with daughter-substitutes. Spooky, or what.

Is it Euros in Gran Canaria?

The phone sits there waiting for me to pick it up and say yes, yes please. But what if *she* answers... If she does I'll ask to speak to dad.

I do Euro signs on a piece of paper while it rings out. The Euro sign can be made into a face if you elongate it to make room for eyes. You can make the two cross-lines into lips and add a nose. Hair is optional.

There's print on it, I pull it out a bit more, might be messing up something important. RyanAir. Two. Wow, dad's sent the tickets already... Cheek, what made him think we were just going to say... no, hang on, Stanstead - Girona. That can't be us.

'Mum... where's Girona?'

She starts and looks round. I feel a tightening in my chest.

'Spain. Yes, they're mine. We're going by ourselves while you're away with dad.'

'But..' He must have... Yeh, right, they talked about it. Course - they discussed it. They're not, like, deadly enemies.

But - she's already got herself and Thinny tickets. What if we'd said no to dad? We nearly did.

Mum would have found a way of getting us to say yes, so she could have love-time with him, on their own. And dad played ball - he'll never come back, now I know for sure. They're working together. Even now. They've joined forces to outwit the kids.

* * *

Before I go on, I want you to read this bit.

*   *   *

Melvin is covered in blood and only just conscious - he keeps drifting out of it, then coming back into the present, then drifting out again. He can see his wife lying still beside him. Melvin knows the bottom of the stairs is not a good place for her to be lying like that, nor himself slumped against the wall. He can't get his thoughts in order.

Anne has a fractured skull and won't survive. She was at the top of the stairs when their district went dark - power cut - carrying a tray down from the bedroom. The sudden darkness threw her, and a milk-jug slid off the tray and broke on the stairs. It was one they'd had as a wedding present. She tried to catch it. In his panic to help her they had both overbalanced and fallen heavily to the bottom.

Falling down the stairs is not that big a deal, especially as Anne was only fifty at the time, Melvin was sixty-four. They were both born on the same day, fourteen years apart. But in a freak mischance the weight of her head came down against the rim of the teapot and both were fractured. If the lights had come back on and gramps had been a bit less dazed she'd have been saved.

I was alive when this happened but not born. Melvin was still working for the brewery, he had six months to go, same as me. They were going on a round the world trip with an insurance policy that would have matured when he was sixty-five, and yielded ten thousand pounds.

She died though, so the policy paid up early. It paid twenty thousand for her death, instead of the ten thousand they would have had if they'd both stayed alive. He paid the cheque into the bank. At home the brochures were still on the table. He stared at them and wept himself to sleep.

It snowed. The following morning his breath was white and there was frost on the inside of the windows. He couldn't eat, couldn't face food, couldn't wash or shave. He fell asleep in the chair. Later he woke up. He forced himself into his coat. He went to the bank. He drew out the twenty thousand pounds. The bank people made him wait, as he was doing something irregular, but he wasn't, and they let him do it.

He cleared the firegrate slowly, placed the brochures carefully, and lit them. It was a fierce blaze. As it died down he fed the twenty thousand one twenty-pound note after another slowly, carefully, like tit-bits to a hungry pet. He waited for each one to burn before tenderly handing it another. Each one was a memory.

* * *

Melvin is gramps, and dad is gramps's son. His job was at the brewery. He shovelled hops into big copper casks where they got boiled and added to the mixture. His father worked in the brewery too. His clothes always smelled of hops even years after he retired. Hops have an earthy, fieldy smell - strong, like tea, but more English and dank grassy.

There was an accident once at the brewery. The big boilers and vats were the same ones that had been used for years, they weren't modern and couldn't be dismantled for cleaning like the new ones can. They only had small openings the size of man-holes in the road, with heavy covers to keep the bacteria out when they were in use. The only way to clean them was to let a small person down inside them. When they were finished they'd bang on the sides to be helped out. The accident happened to Georgio, one of the vat-cleaners. It was very hot weather. The hop smell inside the boiler was so strong it sent him giddy and he lay down in the bottom of the tank for a while and fell asleep. No-one realised he was still in there when they started up the machinery again, and the tank he was in was filled with boiling water and hops and mashed for forty minutes.

When the beer was finished it looked a bit murky but it was certainly full-bodied.

That's a typical gramps story.

I visit gramps loads now, by myself. Grannie Annie, my gran, was his second wife, he was married before. I call her that even though I never knew her, cause gramps talks about her so affectionately. He tells me she was his child-bride. His son from the other marriage lives near Gibraltar, we don't see him.

He doesn't smoke any more, he has started chewing eucalyptus-flavoured tooth-picks to take his mind off it. He chews them all the time and fills ash-trays with them. Disgusting.

He's still a bit crazy after all these years. But now, since Grannie Annie, not just crazy. Deep, too. When the kids put silly hallowe'en masks on and come to the door trick or treating, before he used to have a crazy mask by the door and put it on himself as he was opening it. He would actually scare kids who were there to scare him, and sometimes they would run away. But he's mellowed dad said - he's dad's dad, and Uncle Don's, and Uncle Don's definitely got his loony streak, I can tell you, - what was I on about? Mellowed, yeh, like when fruit goes soft and ripe, that's gramps now. Now, if he could he would come to the door and say 'trick and treat', and let them trick him first then give them money and Maltesers or something. But trick and treaters aren't allowed in his apartments, nor free papers, there's a sign.

* * *

Like I said, the real loony one in our family is dad's brother, Uncle Don. Uncle Don will do anything to make people laugh and is always the one who volunteers when they want someone to come up on stage. One year on holiday they had a beautiful baby contest and for a dare he went in for it as well, a baby's bottle in his mouth with beer in and a towel pinned round his middle with a safety-pin. It made everyone laugh except the babies who all started crying so they had to abandon the contest.

They would probably have cried anyway without the nappy and stuff, cause he just looks scarey. Scarey-crazy. His glasses must have a light-meter or something, they always seem to be reflecting the window-pane it doesn't matter where you are. And he has this weird long chin that goes on for about a foot after his mouth. He looks like a throwback. Surely Grannie Annie didn't.. have.. an aff... My God... Nah, in her photos she's so pretty and gramps is handsome if you can imagine him without Brylcreem and the hair-parting. Anyway, shame on me, I should just accept dad's got a strange-looking brother.

He has a favourite bar, though he goes to several others, where they all know him. He does karaoke nights and sings ballads like he thinks he's Tom Jones, and is in charge on the quiz nights. He has his own place to sit, and when he was thirty they whipped round and got a brass plaque engraved and screwed it to the seat of his stool - 'Don's Arse Goes Here'. It's always shiny where he sits on it.

He's always there ready to talk and laugh with people. He knows how to tell jokes and he can do visual jokes too, making it appear he's broken his nose and things like that. Most kids love him, except Kim and Ry in a way, they'd got him weighed up long before the split and knew if they brought their problems to him he would only make a joke of them. It was their mum, Aunt Rache they went to for help and support.

Aunt Rache married him about thirteen years ago. She says he was the life and soul even then. He was brilliant as well as quite daring. For example, other people would think of having a party at their house, but Uncle Don would hire a boat. Other people would maybe get a D.J., maybe not. Uncle Don would hire a band. Aunt Rache thought he was fabulous, she believed he could do anything. But unfortunately he didn't get excited by ordinary things like fixing a wonky stair - he only got turned on by memorable occasions, and as they got older there weren't so many of them.

*　　　　*　　　　*

Uncle Don's grandest performance of all was at the divorce courts. They moved house to try and patch things up I suppose, but it didn't do any good - made things worse actually cause he said it was too far from his pub, though it wasn't, Ry didn't even need to change schools. It was just being by fields he didn't like, probably thought the sheep were rivals.

The divorce was the greatest show on earth. He contested it in court and defended himself. He made the court staff and public and reporters laugh constantly and had to be told off by the judge, who he addressed as M'Lud, your Holiness, my Esteemed Colleague and things like that. He was in the papers, they loved him, he played the fool for half a day while Aunt Rache faced him across the court in silence and waited her turn. She used to have a recurring dream about a fly, not a house-fly but a beautiful glossy dragon-fly with a turquoise body and two sets of lacey wings. She would feel such a strength of sympathy for it as she watched it hover at the edges of the river bank, that she would almost be the dragon-fly herself, or another one - a sister dragon-fly watching it.

There was a small pier in the dream with some untidy decking, for a boat. It looked neglected. The dragon-fly would move gradually towards it. Aunt Rache would want to call out to warn it of danger, but she wouldn't be able to find her voice. It hovers closer - now its movements are jerky, suddenly, and not pleasant to watch. It is struggling, but there is no creature attacking it.

Aunt Rache adjusts her eyes to the shadow of the pier where the dragon-fly wrestles with something invisible.

It is not strong - it forfeited strength for beauty. Is it being sucked into the water by something?

Then she sees. It has got caught up in a web, a large web, and the more it struggles the more it becomes ensnared. It will not escape, it is large but cannot tear the web.

Aunt Rache moves forward to free it. She can't. She can't move, her arms are pinned to her sides. She is in a web too, all the time she has been watching the web was being spun round her and she's failed to notice. By a big ugly spider, voracious and merciless.

At the end of the case the judge gave her the house, custody of the children and half Uncle Don's pension. She didn't have the dream after that.

Uncle Don was broke.

There was a reporter with a bit of imagination for a story who offered to pay for his life history. Usually reporters have to add bits and pieces to make that kind of thing interesting for the readers, but with Uncle Don they took almost half of it out and still had too much.

After that, for a laugh one of the editors suggested he could run the advice page, answering readers' problems. His advice was very wacky and blokey, and was read by people on building sites. But after a while there were objections from marriage guidance groups and church and stuff saying Uncle Don's answers were setting back all the quiet work they did behind the scenes to encourage respect in marriage and keep couples from splitting up.

The paper eventually let him go, and he went from being a minor celebrity to a loser with hardly any contact with Aunt Rache, Corrie, Kim or Ryan, nowhere decent to live and no dosh.

That was when the spring inside him went ping, and everything came to a stop. He sat on someone's settee for days, smoking and crying to himself. When he'd cried himself out he took himself off to the doctor's and cried some more. They ran a few tests and said his blood wasn't right; he got iron tablets and anti-depressants. Not real iron.

* * *

Sun 12 October

Graham has started moving in.

Slowly at first, clever clever clever, just storing a few things in the baby bedroom which we don't use now.

Then, a couple of weeks later you go in and there's a light-dimmer switch hanging out of the wall. It works, but it's hanging out of the hole in the plaster where it should go, like I imagine an eye if it got gouged out would hang down their face by the veins. It's extremely dangerous, even though he's covered up the bare wires with a piece of black tape. It could come off, it's already curling up at the corners.

Sometimes I imagine I could fix things properly. I'll go to something like a drippy tap and try and unscrew it and fix it. I did that once when dad was still here - well, out, they both were, but still lived here. I got the top of the tap off with a big car spanner. Trouble was, water came gushing out and flooded the floor. I was in a right panic, it's hard screwing a tap-head back on when there's water shooting out.

When I finally sorted it there was water everywhere. I tipped all the dirty washing from the basket on top of it and that soaked it up. Wasn't half heavy when I put it back in though.

Next thing you know he's lugged a whole B & Q workstation in - Graham not dad - and plonked it down in the hallway. He spent ages finding an old shirt and trousers, both dad's, from the garage, and eventually came out about ten o'clock and made himself a coffee. He drank it slowly. Then he had a couple of biscuits, then a glass of orange-juice to take away the taste of the coffee and get the biscuit crumbs out of his teeth, then some water to take away the taste of the orange juice. He slurped it straight from the tap and stood up with a dripping chin which he wiped with his sleeve. He was trying to get himself in the mood by acting rough like he thought builders did.

He sniffed, put his hands on his hips, couldn't think of anything else to distract him, blew his nose and started lugging the parts upstairs. Only they've had a silent committee meeting and voted to resist to the death. When he tries to get them out of the packaging they refuse to co-operate and split his fingernails. After he's assembled it he can't get it in the room. He has to take it all apart and bring each piece in as he needs it, till he's built it in the room. Except it turns out to be too long so he can't fit the top. Then he has to take it down the garage and saw a bit off. Only he's done it crooked so when he puts it together it won't go against the wall properly. He can swear a bit, that's for sure.

By evening he's in. He's installed himself, we didn't even get a vote. The new tom-cat spraying over all your personal places where the lovely warm mellow scents of the old one used to be. All that's left of dad is the rainbow of paint on the garage wall and one partly rebuilt Beetle looking rather sorry for itself - and if he ever dares to touch that...

I'm going to bed.

*   *   *

Saturday 18 Oct @ Maccy D's.

'Hoy Kaz, see that girl's dad…?'

'Where?'

'In front - watch him a min.'

'What's he saying - he's holding everyone up.'

'Listen, you can hear...'

'Um, tell me dear, does that McChicken thing come with new potatoes or chips?'

'Gor, what an idiot.'

'Dad, please - just look at the pictures.'

'Fries sir.'

'Fries? Oh, chips. Yes, well, that's fine for me - what about you two, chips O.K.?'

'Dad please - just a quarter-pounder with fries and Coke.'

'Quarter pounder? I should have thought they'd be doing it all in metric by now, that's what you learn in school isn't it?'

'DAD...'

'Coke with yours sir, or Tango or Sprite?'

'Sprite... sounds like some sort of forest nymph doesn't it... I wonder if I could have a cup of Earl Grey tea instead? Lemon rather than milk, no sugar.'

'Cor Kim, fancy having that for your dad.'

'*Please* dad, just have a Coke and sit down.'

'Now that's why all you kids get bad teeth - I doubt there's a single child here who can stand up and say they haven't got a filling...'

'No Old Grey tea sir. Coke, Tango or Sprite.'

'*Earl* Grey, not old. What exactly's in this Sprite stuff then?'

'Dunno sir, just Sprite. D'you want it or not?'

'Dad, *please*. Yes. Yes, he does. Just shuttup dad, don't say anything.'

* * *

{The girl who is pleading with her dad goes to private school. Her name is Heidi. Kim knows her. Her dad left when she was four and her brother was a baby, they only see him in contact times. He hasn't got a clue how seriously he embarrassed his kids on that day. After, they didn't see so much of him, they made up a few excuses like feeling sick and things. Their mum realised and didn't make them go if they didn't want to. Their dad complained, but not too much.

Forget it now, you'll meet her later.}

* * *

Sun 19 October

Have you noticed something? There are some serious wackos on the <u>male</u> side of our family. Shaun and dad aren't so bad, but if I had to give the rest a loony rating out of ten I would give gramps eight, Ryan nine and Uncle Don a straight ten, he's off the scale.

Ryan is Uncle Don's son - our cousin and Shaun's numero uno buddy. He is quite naughty. He is allowed in the street and park quite a lot and swears when he gets told off at home. He is always on a warning at school, and recently my Aunt Rache and her current bloke were told he had to improve or they would be asking him to find another school.

Ryan has a pet snake, given by Uncle Don after the split-up. It was the perfect present for him, and also perfect for sending Aunt Rache round the twist, like giving a hyperactive kid in a flat with violent neighbours a steel drum set. Uncle Don's good at things like that. Nasty things disguised as nice things, basically. It spends most of the day sleeping in its tank and livens up at night. It has a dim red light for night-times and Ry listens to it rustling around as he drops off to sleep. He feeds it meat scraps and sometimes finds frogs for it.

When dad went, Shaun crumpled a bit to be honest, and Ry enrolled him on a course of naughtiness (which Ry was the senior teacher of). Shaun was a bit of a borderline student, but Ry did manage to get him to pay me back for bossing him and acting too much like a grown-up. He made my bed for me and told me he'd put a hot water bottle in. Actually it was Betty, Ry's tortoise, he'd put her down there with a few lettuce leaves, so there was more chance of her leaving a deposit of poops. Sweet.

Ryan's day of glory at school came when they let him bring his python in. Hargreaves was detailed to accompany him around the classes. Hargreaves is a quick wiry little guy but he still couldn't stop it swallowing Laura Hill's watch. After that Ry turned his attention back to his battle to the death with MacAlie, Britain's meanest teacher, doing little guffs in the class and things like that just to keep her on a permanent state of alert.

He's the only kid I know of who actually likes the dentist, it reminds him of a mortuary where dead bodies go, with the light shining fiercely in your face on the end of a strange long clamp that bends like an arm, and x-rays of people's skulls on a light-box on the wall, with teeth showing. The dentist comes with a hypodermic needle full of liquid and makes you open really wide, like the places where they strap you down and do experiments in James Bond films. We've just got to hope Ry never becomes one, that's all.

* * *

Actually, something quite drastic is happening to Ry, he's gone all hip-hop and weird. He always used to go round doing voices but we didn't listen much, just presumed he had a little phantom friend like kids do. He used to go round the house doing Kyle and Cartman till Aunt Rache caught him saying, 'They killed Kenny, bastards...' and slapped him. Then he did 'Hey, eat ma shorts' and all the Bart Simpson stuff. It made a lot of kids in his class laugh, especially Shaun, till they realised Colin Jones could do him better. And Homer. They put a dead bird in his tray for stealing the limelight.

But now he's moved on to Ali G, and it's more than just imitating, it's like a major personality change. Funny the way people change, like Kim and me - I never questioned she was the leader but she's not any more, it's maybe fifty-fifty, or even a bit more me. I can't tell, except I know it's different from before. Like getting boobs I suppose, you can never exactly say when it started. Just starts. Anyway, it's the same with Ry, first he was just a kid with a python in his room, now he's this crazy little groover.

His room's gone cool for one thing. It's all West Ham stuff, first time I saw it had changed I thought it was Villa, then recognised some of the players. Even his pillow-case and duvet are claret and blue. I asked Shaun why West Ham, because no-one in either of our families is London. He said Bobby Moore once ruffled Uncle Don's hair. I said Bobby Moore's dead. He says, 'So is Jesus, doesn't stop people going to church does it.' I said, 'Don't get cheeky with me,' and he middle-fingered me and walked out. Walked. Him as well... we're all changing, must be the local water. Didn't half scamper up the stairs though.

It was Ry's idea to start ringing people up. I think they just both wanted to ring their dads basically, but you can't can you, it's such a shame being a boy and I don't mean that in a nasty way. But it's nearly always the dad who goes, and they either think they can't ring cause it's outside his agreed contact times or bottle out in case they get told the truth: 'I don't want you, you belong to your mother now, I got the C.D.'s.' I really don't know how it goes with split-ups. They always say they love *you*, it's just mum they can't even sit in the same room with. But they said they loved her to start with, when they wanted to get married, so how do we know?

Anyway, they never got round to their dads, Ry and Shaun, they started ringing other people. Any other people. They'd just grab the phone-book and start flicking through till they found a suitable name.

'Let's see... Parsons, Tomkinson, Toyland, Wilson. Toyland, that's a decent one... Hello? Mrs Toyland?'

'Speaking.'

'It's Big Ears here, how ya diddlin?'

'Pardon?'

'BIG EARS. What's up, deaf or something. I've got Noddy with me, put the kettle on, we'll be round in five.'

'Who is that? Is that you Joseph?'

'Better make that three, we've got P.C. Plod an' all. Get a bloody move on then, we haven't got all day.'

'Get off the line before I call my husband.'

'Tata Toyland, time to go.' Brrrrr.

I would say ninety-five percent of my mates, including me, don't have a clue if they're loved or not, and don't even know if love has rules or if it's just what you feel like at the time. I mean I love Mars Bars, but I soon get fed up of scoffing them. So my opinion is love's no big deal, it just tastes nice if you get my meaning. But after that there are things like looking out for each other plus your kids. Always. But as soon as people have to do something for someone they start hating the person.

It started after West Ham sold one of their best players, the phoning, and Ry was really annoyed.

'They're just trying to make money out of him,' he said. 'You might make a bit on the transfer, but it's no good if you get stuck in the Nationwide is it?'

'Nine million's more than a bit,' Shaun said.

'It's friggin peanuts,' he snapped. 'Come on, let's find the bugger and tell him what we think. They should listen to the fans.'

'How? Get on a train and go and shout his name out in... what's the place where he's gone?'

'No idiot, get the phone book and start ringing up.' He snatched it up off the floor. There were about twelve with the same name. He found one with the right initial and started dialling. Couldn't possibly be him, it was only the local book for a start.

'Hello..? Listen, Judas, blokes like you make me sick. Money money money, that's all you think about, you're useless anyway we don't need you. GET LOST.'

He slammed the phone down. Imagine some poor bloke sat in his kitchen trying to pick the bits out of that, I wished I could have seen him.

My cousin Corrie - that's Kim's sister - went out with a boy called Javed for a bit, till his dad stopped it. He stopped it cause Javed's wife's already been chosen and he's got to marry her when she's old enough. His dad probably didn't want him getting a taste for the sweet things that don't nourish you. Like Mars Bars... Clever how I put that. Anyway, what's the big deal about arranged marriages, maybe it would be better if your family chose for you. All our family chose for themselves and it didn't do much good, so, whatever... Mind I'd die if someone chose Simon Cauldwell for me.

'Your turn now.'

'O.K. - um... Parsons, Pedle...' Bip bip dib dib dip dip dip tip... 'Hello Mister Pedle, how about a piddle...' Brrrr.

'That's no good, do it properly. Here, give us the book... Adams, Ainsley... Ali. Hey - Ali, A - B - F ... G! Ali G...'

'Hello, who is please?'

'Mister Ali..?'

'Gulam Ali sir, how may I help?'

'Hey man - mi Ali G too man. Buyaka Sha.'

'Sir?'

'Mi Ali G. Mi like writin poems man, mi sit on de tailet where dem cyan' 'terrupt me. You wanna hear ona mi poems?'

'It would be a pleasure, sir...'

'O.K. man, dis 'bout mi fam'ly an fings:

Mi got two sister bu' mi no gat no brudder,
Wi dad dun left whome, bu' wi still got wi mudder,
Mi hate mi teacha, dis lady she not pleasin,
Her shoutin at dem boys man when dem givin her no reasin.

Dat mi favorit man. Wha'ya say?'

'You have most particular talent sir...'

'Hey. You mi brudder, wi twins innit? Maximum respect. Buyaka Sha.'

'You are welcome sir.'

*　　　*　　　*

Thursday October 23rd

Ryan has got himself in the local paper, front page. With MacAlister. No - they're not getting married. Nope - he didn't propose her for Teacher of the Year. He got clobbered by her and got himself suspended, they both are actually, her as well for hitting a kid. Hah! MacAlie suspended... MacAlie needs naughty kids to make her feel like a crusader for good, so Ryan obliged. Mind you Ry's a bit special, he'd be naughty if he was in the same class as Jesus and Nelson Mandela. Trouble is, good little kids like Shaun start adjusting to her wavelength as well. She keeps telling them she knows what they're up to, so in the end they get up to things. They're embarrassed for her. They want her to be right.

MacAlie's fighting dirty and says Ry is making it up. Aunt Rache is standing by him, but you can tell she's not sure. Ry is a little beggar but he wouldn't make that kind of stuff up, no way, it wouldn't come into his head. He likes niggling teachers, that's all, one-on-one's his thing. Probably thought she liked it too till she clocked him and sent him home with his ears ringing - as in, liked having a little brat around to soak up her bad moods for her. It's hard for him now, being accused of making things up to destroy her career. Hard for Shaun too. Shaun trusts people basically, he doesn't get it.

Anyway, half-term now, maybe things will blow over.

*　　　　　*　　　　　*

(Still Thursday, after supper)

Right. Well, after all that lot before about the looney types on the men side of the family, let's calm down and have a nice girley chapter about us from the feminine side.

Corrie is Kim and Ry's sister, she's my other cousin and you could say she's a bit mad, but she's lovely-mad, not crazy-mad. It would be hard to describe her cause she has a different look about every two months. I've seen her with all colours of hair, and any length from dreadlocks to almost none. Studs and pins everywhere to no studs, just plain and innocent. Well, as innocent as she can look, usually the image is slightly overshadowed by burgundy toe-nails or passion-flower lipstick not to mention the odd tattoo. But her basic look is a small pretty brunette with energy and a bit of attitude, something between Natalie Umbruglia and Pink.

She was like a mum to me and Kim when we were small. Smaller. Mum and Aunt Rache were the looking-after mums - they fed us and potty-trained us and took us to the clinic for jabs. But Corrie was our street-mum: she taught us everything you have to know to get along in life. She was our survival tutor, and lecturer in the ways of the world. Mum and Aunt Rache taught us to be polite, Corrie taught us to be tough.

She was always up for it, always the first: she cheeked teachers at school and got punishments. If she got an after-schooler Kim would have to lie for her, say she'd stopped for drama practice and things like that. Corrie always got away with it.

She was the first to date a boy and snog him properly. She was twelve. She shouted out at the head-teacher in assembly cause he blamed the netball team for letting the school down by losing a match they should have won - just stood up off the floor and shouted, 'You weren't there, so how do you know if we gave up or not. Anyway, it's only a game, you should be thinking about our education not netball.'

She was a hero. Even some of the teachers gave her little smiles and nods for what she did - they talked and laughed about it for days in the staffroom and asked themselves why they hadn't got the courage to answer him back when he got pompous.

Javed was her first proper boyfriend. Good-looking in a kind of proud Asian way. Still lives round here. He was wary of girls then. Wary of boys too probably, never sure if he would be greeted or insulted. Corrie knew these things. She was curious. She watched him a few times when the other kids wouldn't notice. He seemed gentle. The fact that people might wind her up for liking a local Paki boy set off a kind of defiance in her, and she made the decision she would try. That's what she's like, I worshipped her. Still do, actually.

When she was doing her hair-styling course at college the lecturer asked her on a date and she went even though she was only sixteen. She did outrageous hairstyles on herself and her friends. Aunt Rache threatened to kick her out a couple of times. She also had piercings and her first tattoo. Aunt Rache knew about the piercings, but had no idea about the tattoo, which was very well hidden, she wouldn't have even known where to start looking...

After the thing with the hair-styling lecturer she quit the course, and she and her friend set up a business together doing party-plan - costume jewellery and accessories - and it's still going now. They have their own company car with lettering on.

She is a brilliant dancer.

*   *   *

Kim can be a little bitch. She knows I can run a bit and I know she can. We're the two best in school, in relay our team won the District with a new record. I was third leg and she was fourth. I remember how we all put our arms round each other for the paper - pity it didn't get printed really - and looked so friendly.

But the camera can lie.

For example, the sports teacher in our school is Mr Benson who is seriously fat. Baldy Benson, he plays rugby: he's one of the shove-and-grunt brigade, when they do that all-hold-on-and-shove-the-other-lot-with-your-head thing. Scrum. Benson could scrum an elephant, he's got ears like one too, big floppy pink things.

Kim flirts with him. It's true, the little bitch, we all know she does it. 'Suirr...' in her girly flirty dirty voice, 'could I help you with the equipment sir..?' Going on about floor mats but using a voice as if to say, sir sir you're so big and handsome I really want to marry you please wait for me to grow up...

And he falls for it, silly old git, that's how she got to be in the paper holding up the District trophy with a foxy England triallist from our local running club instead of it being all four of us with our arms round.

Kim is the world's outright top gossip, she's got eyes like an eagle, ears like a cat, and she knows how to fill in the gaps if you see what I mean. As well as a good runner she is quite tough, and she can ride horses. But she's mellowed since they put her out for a couple of days in year three for nicking one of Miss Lynton's fags and pretending to smoke it. Kim was the leader of us two going back as far as I can remember, she was number one and I was number two, though we never ever said. But I've had a feeling recently it's beginning to change. I can't exactly put a finger on it, just a feeling.

* * *

She hasn't got the Uncle Don chin by the way, it would serve her right if she did though - if it grew a bit longer every time she told a porky or exaggerated something. Nor has Ry, well, maybe a bit, you hardly notice but I suppose there's plenty of time for it to grow. I would describe her as beautifully lively rather than beautiful looking. I would say she would be quite plain with fair not blonde hair, blue eyes and some freckles but a bigger than average nose. She would be plain if she was the serious type, but she's not, she's always talking and when she does her expressions are amazing. She also has graceful movements not just in discos but also clumsy places like the long-jump pit where other kids sprawl on their bums like upturned beetles and show their kegs to everyone. I suppose that's riding horses for you, gives you natural balance.

Aunt Rache is their mum, hers and Ry's, and Corrie's. She's... well, Aunt Rache is Aunt Rache. She's about three years younger than mum but they've always got on really well. They've been divorced about four years I think, her and Uncle Don. She is still pretty but in a more sort of hesitating way than before, not so up for it, but her hair is a very striking blonde and though she goes through the changes with men there is always another one on the cards.

*   *   *

Well, that's us I suppose, Corrie, Kim and Aunt Rache, plus me and mum. Funny there seems to be loads more to say about the men than us, I wonder if wackos are more interesting to people. Reading about them I mean, not living with. There's only Corrie really, who I would give about six on the wacky scale, but she's not a proper wacko, just out-front and daring.

*   *   *

Friday 24th of Oct

'Don't tell anyone till I say, right...'

'Ay?'

'They don't want anyone to know yet in case she doesn't get on.'

'What? On what?'

'Corrie might be on Big Brother.'

'WOW!! When? How come..?'

'Just phoned the number and they got her to send a bit of a video and stuff - then she got chosen for an interview. And now she's gone through to the last fifty.'

'Wow. How do they choose?'

'Dunno, have to do some trials or something...'

'Don't forget to tell me what happens.'

That will mean two media stars if Corrie gets selected. First Uncle Don's column in the papers, what was it called..? 'Don Deliberates', that's it. It was the biggest load of rubbish. Someone wrote in and said her husband had tipped their dining table over with the Sunday lunch on and stormed out, she was going out of her mind. His advice was 'Try putting more salt in the potatoes'. Silly idiot, he had the time of his life writing them. And now Corrie if she gets in. She'd definitely win it.

'...Trouble is, Dave's got a *criminal record,* so they might not have her if they find out.'

'Wow, what's he done? Banks?'

'Nup. Drove the wrong way up a one-way street. Really fast.'

'Very funny. That doesn't make him a criminal.'

'It does. The police are going to persecute. He might get sent to prison.'

'No way.'

'Corrie says she'll stay faithful even if he gets life.'

'Ah, that's really nice.'

* * *

Tues 28th Oct

Canaria. Hot. Shaun staring hard at the pool where the squeals and shouts are coming from. He's got dad now but can't compete with Carol.

'Six Euros for a Telegraph? It's a rip-off. Here you are - why d'you want it, anyway, it's a Tory paper...'

Funny dad. Carol sits up to see where the shadow's coming from. Topless.

I snatch the money and run. Funny clever dad. Not sexy but topless. I hate big newspapers, they've never got anything about the soaps and stuff. But there's a whole page weather forecast on the back with a map of Europe, I noticed. Ignoring the fronts and pressure things I go straight to the temperatures. G - Girona. Not there. Work up from the bottom.. W - Warsaw, but that's Poland or somewhere. Croatia? Where's near? Try from the top down like normal people do. Barcelona - can't be far, it's Spain. Sun, twenty-eight degrees. An image of mum by another pool looking gorgeous for the first time in years swims before my eyes for a second or two, before diving down and dragging me with it, down to the bottom of the deep end. Funny thing sadness, people don't always see it specially if they aren't looking. It hasn't made my tan go green or anything, it looks fine, just fine.

I refold it and go back to tanning, to dad's bemusement. It's horrible seeing your own parent as a lover, it shouldn't happen don't ask me why. My back is burning but I stay flat. If I roll over he'll feel he's got to put on his father's face and ask if we're O.K. And she'll be there leaning her pink girley boobs on his shoulder staring in her not-motherly way.

Poor Shaun, he hates the sun, just goes red. He's a kind brother but not very daring, he stays off school sick a lot if he gets a cold or sore throat. Never used to, maybe he wants to be mum's little boy again, mum and dad's little boy, or maybe his first junior teacher came as a bit of a shock to him. Mind, talk about baptism of fire - she'd be a shock to Lennox Lewis, MacAlie.

MacAlie, horrible gaunt face and tight mouth, staring glaring specs. Aunt Spiker - in her frocks that look like used parachutes where her boobs should be.

MacAlie picks on boys. Boys aren't so good at tricking adults, and Shaun's no different. He can lie good nowadays but can't do cute faces and stuff. If a boy does a cute face and smiles when an adult asks something they think he's taking the mick.

The only time he really got mad about the split-up - they had something on Holyoaks where the boy smashes all the lights on his dad's car with a baseball bat, and Shaun must have decided that as dad wasn't there, that was the tactic to use on mum. He had this massive temper tantrum, it was major, even I was scared, only there wasn't a baseball bat to hit her with. He hunted everywhere for something. In the end he had to get her to help him. 'Will this do?' she was saying, trying her best to find something.

I never wanted to mother him through his bad patch he should toughen up and get a life, but hey, can't let him cook, poor kid. I tap his shoulder and challenge him to table footer. He flinches, god, didn't realise he was that tense, and says no sharply. I rummage for my Jacqueline Wilson but there's a shadow. He's up.

'Alright then.'

Dad grabs for his trousers. 'Do you need money?', and she goes for her bag in unison like the loyal underling.

'Got some,' he says without turning round.

He's blue, I'm red. I'm on the ball-side which means I have to take my hand off the rods a minute to push it in. His head dropped in concentration, lips pursed, he swivels the rods like a maniac not following the ball properly, but bashes a goal anyway and punches in triumph. I drop it in again. Same thing - he's at it so aggressively the table legs are rocking and it's making the ball roll crooked, mostly to his players.

'Shaun...'

'Shut up, play to win or I'm going...'

I try and concentrate. It's hard. I know if I let him get another one he'll blow his top cause I do it like a girl, but if I get one he'll blow his top cause I played as hard as him and humiliated him.

It comes to my goalie again, I slide the thing up and back hoping to get lucky. It wedges itself under the foot and stays on the goal-line. He swings round in disappointment as if he's a real player and has just narrowly missed. I'm trying to free it when it seems to flip out by itself and roll tamely all the way through the players to his goal before he can get his hands back on.

'You cheat!' he shouts, banging the glass, making people look from their papers, 'play by yourself, I'm going ho...'

He stops just in time. For a second his angry face goes desperate, then he turns and stomps off to the apartment.

The hot days pass and the breathless nights intruded by shouts, snatches of music and mosquitoes. On our last night it must be the end of a festival and there is the sudden whistle of rockets and huge coloured dandelion clocks crackle and fill the sky and fade and fill it again for ages.

* * *

Saturday 1st of November

We're tucked in our Easyjet seats pointing home. Silver fuselage, silver wings, gleaming. Way under, French people silently farm yellow squares and inch along roads. I look across the blue blue, scanning the horizon - I think for a glimpse of another plane coming from the south-east... Yes, it doesn't take much effort to fantasise mum's plane cruising up alongside us and heading to England together. Out of my window I see her, she's in exactly the same seat her side and we smile a radiant mother-daughter smile to each other and give a little wave.

The captain's voice snaps me out of it.

'Ladies and gentlemen we are expecting a little turbulence, please fasten seat-belts, extinguish all hopes and get real.'

Who? What..?

We're nearly there, back down to earth.

*　　*　　*

Monday 3rd Nov

School starts again, everyone in the playground's like - wow, lovely tan, lucky you. Actually I do feel quite lucky - luckier - mum's like a cloud's passed over at last, bit sickly with him, Graham, but much much softer. She's putting on weight, too, you can see a right little pot belly on her in the photos, that's contentment for you. I'm so glad, it made me feel helpless when she was miserable.

Also Ry is back, all they've done is move him to Benson's class. I suppose you'd have to say Aunt Rache has adjusted, I never thought I'd live to see the day. Adjusted to MacAlister's lies about her son, and accepted that it's best to just let him be moved to another class. Aunt Rache is on at him to be grateful he didn't get dumped among the bullies at the other place a bus ride away. Actually he probably is fairly chuffed, Benson's a decent swap if you ask me - Ry plays up and they give him a better teacher. It's Shaun who's the unlucky one, he never did a thing and they've separated him from his best mate.

We're in Miss Stanislaus's class and it's totally quiet. It's reading time. Miss Stanislaus does loads of reading time and gets really good books, she buys them with her own money if she can't get them from school or the library. Miss Stanislaus is a belter. And she likes the boys. If you've ever been in juniors recently you'll know the girls get the attention, boys get the telling-offs, it's a rule of life. But not in Miss Stanislaus's they don't. Boys get at least the same, maybe more, and we don't mind. She's popular with all the kids, we gossip about who she loves out of the other teachers but no-one believes it cause there are only two men teachers and they're both old and married. She has got a boyfriend actually, his name is Brian and he is a P.E. teacher at the High School where we're going soon. They've been on holiday together, so it's quite serious.

Miss Stanislaus's best characteristic is, she's impatient. Not in the way of telling people off if they don't work, but in the way of doing things she says she'll do. If someone in class tells her about a good book she'll say, 'I'll get that...', which with some adults means they won't and with others means they'll get it in three months, when you've got fed up of waiting and can't be bothered any more. If Miss Stanislaus says she'll get something or do something, she means next day, and she never lets anyone down.

The nearest I can describe her is a sort of young black-haired Zoe Ball, a real ladette who knows loads about football, garage and dance music, clubbing, and fellas. She has a smart blue Peugeot 206. She makes us all feel like we're eighteen and ready to take the world by storm, I can't wait. She is the best. She has shiny dark curly hair tumbling down onto her shoulders, lovely dark skin, big soft brown eyes and a really beautiful figure. She wears expensive clothes, always dark colours, and jewellery. She's like a star, all us kids adore her, the boys check what she's wearing as much as the girls. She has a quiet voice and a mysterious smile, as if she knows secrets, and in a way she does. She knows the secrets of her homeland, the place where her parents grew up, a remote place where the sun bakes the olive trees all day and snakes and lizards crouch in cracks.

Kim will do anything for her - she stays in at lunch-times to help her (and listen to her conversations on the mobile, which are often to people on the Continent). She's like me with Corrie, she practically dreams about her.

Doesn't stop her gossiping about her though, nothing would, she's the kind of school News of the World snoop - way ahead of the pack, and take my word for it, there is a pack, all spying on Miss Stani's every move, and anyone else's, and broadcasting exclusives.

* * *

We get called to a special assembly.

'Hey Kaz, look at MacAlister, she doesn't just scowl at kids when they talk, she scowls at the other teachers as well.'

'Yeh - wonder if she keeps them in at play.'

Actually it's Miss Stanislaus MacAlie's staring at for being too friendly with us kids - she's letting the ones at the end of the line tell her about their holiday. And adding to her crime by smiling instead of shouting at them.

'Nah, they stay in anyway, she prob'ly kicks them out.'

'She'd have a job kicking Baldy out...'

'Yeh, like a barn door isn't he. Ry's not complaining though... Shh, she's looking.'

Our little assembly gossip gets cut off by the head coming in. It's not very good organisation, there's still only two classes in, ours and Shaun's, maybe the rest haven't had the message. There's a gap of about four rows between us but the head ignores it and starts in his confiding voice. I feel the hairs on my neck, something's going to happen. As he talks I look at Miss Stanislaus and then at MacAlie who are both staring dead in front of them, and don't tell me how - I know. He's swapping our teachers.

I get a tinny taste in my mouth, and by the time the rest of them gasp in astonishment my head's swimming with shock and awareness, and anger. This is my awareness: neither of the teachers wants to swap. Miss Stanislaus has had her class stolen off her for no reason, and I know she liked us, she really did, now she's got to start again with littlies. And MacAlie is being punished for what she did, so she gets foisted with us biggies. And that's my anger: they don't believe her. So what's her punishment for lying and humiliating my aunt and her family? Sack? No, she keeps her job, we're the ones who get sacked, from our wonderful, lovely teacher and our wonderful teacher gets sacked from her lovely class. Cause we are, we're a well-O.K. class, we'll adjust to anything. MacAlie gets us instead, pif-paf-poof, just like that. Her reward for Services to Untruth.

We file in silently, from shock, not her. I just catch a glimpse of the bleak expression on Miss Stanislaus's face as she shuts the door on her new mini-class, twitching and whispering excitedly. As they go in to our room.

It gets worse. The tables are in rows, and most of the displays are down from the walls. You'd think they could have swapped, then at least there'd have been some familiar things for us to come into, but it's bare.

She talks to us like we're all four and a half and have hearing difficulties. 'Who else would like to be a nurse and save soldiers' lives like Florence Nightingale, hmm children?' Do us a favour, the girls all want to be J-Lo and the boys want to be Wayne Rooney. I'd be Faye from Steps myself if I couldn't be Corrie, I don't care if they were naff, she was the greatest. I wonder what she's doing now. Is she secretly making a solo album that's going to suddenly explode onto the market and blow Kylie away - or is she just taking time out to be a brilliant mum?

I get home at the end of a very long day.

Kim's really angry about it too but she adjusts quicker than me, I suppose she can't complain too much, Ryan being in the middle of it all. Besides, it would take more than a teacher-swap to stop her cascade of gossip, I doubt if a world war would do it.

'Hey Kaz, heard about Mr Hargreaves?'

'Yeh, won a million quid on Millionaire.'

'Pig. Well, it is about money, sort of. He doesn't just work here..'

'Very good Kim, that's right, he goes home to his little wifey and kiddy-winks when it gets dark, doesn't he...'

'Dick-face - he's got another job as well, part-time. Wanna know what he does? I suppose you know that as well do you?'

'Midget in a circus?'

'Chicken-beaker.'

'Ay?'

'That got you. Chicken-beaker. They clip chickens' beaks so they don't peck themselves. You know what that means, don't you?'

'No rumpy-pumpy in the mating season. "Give us a little peck henny, I'm in the mood for lurve..." '

'Very witty. It means he could have brought bird flu into this school. What if it lies dormant till the next outbreak, you can't be sure.'

'They'll have to burn our carcasses. Suits me, I don't think I can take another day of MacAlie.'

'If you're not gonna be serious...'

* * *

God I didn't realise how lucky I've been up till now..... I'm one of those kids who's actually always liked school. Of course I didn't tell anyone and I played up teachers sometimes, especially Lynto in year three, but actually I thought getting to paint every week, do gym and P.E., watch hamsters have babies and frogspawn turn to taddies was great. And you get decent dinners. It's O.K., worth suffering a bit of maths for.

Now Shaun and Ry like it all of a sudden and I'm the dweeb who can't get on.

I expect Hargreaves does do that chicken-pecker thing. He's one of these blokes who can always get people something on the Q.T. There's been a rumour for ages (started if I remember by Kim) that Sanitary Services at the market has quite a lot of repackaged stock if you get where I'm coming from. But I don't think anyone would challenge him openly about that, not even the head, cause he has a 24/7 minder, Sophie.

Sophie. Now here's one real wacko lady character just to show we can be if we want.

Sophie is a dog with an obesity problem. In human sizes she would be size eighteen. She is a labrador who looks more like a bear. She is Hargreaves's dog and her job is to keep strangers out of our school but she just goes up to them wagging her tail. When it wags the whole of her backside sways from side to side too. She eats two cans of Butchers Boy a day and supplements them with morsels from the playground, such as bits of sandwich the kids chuck down, plus the odd bluebottle or wasp she manages to catch if it flies too close to her nose. She washes it down with puddle water. She is also quite partial to salt and vinegar crisps, prawn cocktail, plain, barbeque chicken, any flavour, she's not that fussy. She eats the wrappers as well cause she can't get her shout far enough inside to lick the grease. She ate Aaron's trainer he left in the playground, but spat out the lace.

She's ninety-seven dog years. Huge pink belly with nipples all the way down. Big chomping mouth like a horse's, it has short white hair around it. And a saggy back where Hargreaves's children used to have rides on her. Till they were about twelve.

I would give Sophie nine and a half on the wacko scale.

*   *   *

Where was I? Oh yeh, Shaun and Ry. They charge in the kitchen together talking about it. Ry talking about school, I don't believe it. His lot have had music. Baldy lets them take turns on instruments. Can't play anything but they rattle and shake em. Big sticks with bells on, and cymbals. There was a fight over cymbals so the two halves got split up - one kid went off with his half thumping it with the fluffy drumstick-thing and the other kid went somewhere else to thump his half. Never occurred to them to wait a bit then join forces again.

Never occurred till Ry makes his move. He gets one and holds it up for another kid to bash with a stick with bells. There's a massive great dwanging boom, bells fly off everywhere and the kid's left holding the plain stick with about three left on, like a conker tree branch after it's had a few bricks chugged up at it.

'Taylor, Simpson - staffroom.'

'But sir, we were doing a storm.'

'I'll be doing a storm in a minute. Desert Storm. Go on - NOW.'

*   *   *

Still Monday (longest day of my life)

I go and visit gramps, there's no-one else. Mum's in cuckoo-land with Graham, dad's impossible to have a serious conversation with and Kim's adjusted.

He's got some good mates there, three are ex-policemen and they have a lot of laughs together. The residents play cards and board-games, and when they get the Cluedo board out they make the ex-cops play for a joke. He gets me to tell about what happened with Ryan.

'She needs stringing up,' one of them says, but they don't get too worked up, they've seen it all before. Injustice. Dying before you're ready to go, that's the only injustice that concerns them now - a kid moaning about her teacher doesn't make the start-line.

'Keep your head up and look them in the eye - like your grandad does, my sapphire - he's the one to follow...'

I ask if he means anything, or is it just a compliment. Gramps dismisses it. He gets out of his chair and leads me to the veranda. We look at the grounds. There are the last of the flowers, blood red and yellow leaves, a squirrel scampering and stopping. The sun is low and weak, stretching the tree shadows right across. Winter is coming, the garden hedges are covered in silver webs some mornings and your shoes get wet from the grass. Gramps tells me about the day he first arrived and was shown to his room and left to collect his thoughts and arrange his things.

It was completely bare, except for a picture of a lake on the wall and a bible. He sat on his bed thinking about all the old times seeing his whole life shrivelled up into a hard wrinkled pea.

There was a knock on the door and it opened itself - no waiting for him to answer here; the top lady whatever she was called filled the doorway smartly.

'Time to meet the others Mr Taylor...'

The dreaded moment when he would walk into the lounge to be scrutinised by all the rest.

In the doorway he looked round slowly, meeting the gazes, looking for a spare chair to sit on. There was only one, right across the room, furthest from the door. He made his way across the carpet with its brown and green swirls like sinking sand trying to suck him in and drag him under.

There was a terrible silence. The eyes followed him speechlessly, no-one spoke or coughed. Only the heaviness of their breath accompanied him. But he kept his head up, eyes on the chair. 'I am entitled to be here,' he thought, 'they won't defeat me.'

From the corridor a trolley rattled along bringing tea, and the atmosphere loosened a little. The lady next to him finally leaned over to speak.

'Mrs Hopkins always sat there,' she said in a whisper, 'but she died yesterday. Died right in the chair and they had to lift her out of it.'

Gramps had been given the Chair of Doom.

* * *

This time it wasn't one of his wacky stories, it was the truth, and we were both quiet for a long time after. In my silence I was thinking he was right to burn all that money, I don't know what he was thinking in his silence. I remember mum said dad and Uncle Don were very angry with him, especially Uncle Don who was always looking for easy ways to make money. They claimed he was unhinged with grief and tried to get the bank to admit he shouldn't have been allowed to withdraw it. They wanted it to be replaced. But he stopped them.

I stared at the trees a long time, the sun was only on some of them now.

'It wasn't yours to spend, was it gramps,' I said, half to myself, thinking we'd talked the bit in my head.

'No,' he said after a think. 'I couldn't have betrayed her like that.'

We were quiet again. Gramps doesn't rush, but when he does something, he is absolutely sure. He never moved away from the Chair of Doom, although there were plenty of chances to after. It was in the best spot, for one thing. It was a chair to him, just a flat piece with legs holding it off the floor and a back, he refused to give it a character. If the others wanted to spook themselves it was their affair.

* * *

Fri 7th November

Another reason for Miss Stanislaus to be mad, she had organised an author for the day, and got loads of his books so we could all have a good read of them first - now her new class, Shaun's, are too young so The Liar gets him instead. The Liar never organised anything in her life except detentions and maybe a quick getaway on the last day of term. I feel like going in with a placard like they do at the football when they've got sick of the manager. 'MACALISTER OUT - DUMP THE LIAR'. Not very fair on Shaun though, he's like a kid reborn. He's talking about school all the time now. And another thing, only a small thing, he laughs about himself getting answers wrong and making mistakes. Like when Miss Stani reads to them he puts his thumb in his mouth and hums to himself. The other day she stopped in the middle and said, who's humming? And he looked round to see who it was and was surprised to see the other kids pointing at him. He hadn't been aware he was doing it.

She has also dealt with the little gang of informers The Liar had established. This is how she dealt with one of the chief ones, an obnoxious sucking-up cutie with tight lips - she'd heard Ry and some of the others, Shaun no doubt, being gross outside. I love Miss for this, I could hear every word when Shaun told us.

'Please miss, some boys swore in the playground.'

'What did they say Victoria?'

'Rude words miss.'

'What words...'

'Can't say miss.'

'I won't know whether they're rude unless you tell me.'

'They are miss.'

'How do you know?'

'My parents told me never to say them.'

'How did they tell you?'

'Miss..?'

'What did they say when they told you?'

'Don't say those words miss. Ever.'

'What words?'

'Don't know miss.'

'Well, did they say them to you?'

'No way miss, my parents never swear.'

'So how did you know what words they meant?'

'Don't know miss.'

'Go and sit down for now...'

Hah! Brilliant. I miss her like stink. Sometimes I hear a little passage of her lovely soft voice coming down the corridor when her door's open, and it practically overwhelms me.

*　　　*　　　*

Still Fri 7th - the author.

We listened to the author's stories and laughed, me and Kim laughing together, we laughed like we were on our own having a private joke, but loudly with the rest, too. We laughed at the dog he brought with him, yawning on the stage, more than the author himself, whose stories are quite boring. When it comes to questions all the kids ask him about himself and his dog, instead of his stories.

He hasn't got any children - well, he has but he doesn't know where they live or how old they are, from his marriage about thirty years ago. He just has his dog called Gip, and he takes him round to schools and festivals with him. Sometimes they allow him to bring Gip in and sometimes not, so he spends the day in the car and goes mad when the author finally opens it up to let him out. If they let him come in the author puts his blanket down in the hall by his chair with a bowl of water and Gip sits or lies there ignoring the children. He takes great sloppy gulps from the bowl in the middle of the author's stories and the kids all laugh. Just as he was telling us this a bee buzzed past Gip's nose and he suddenly leapt up barking and chased it. Everyone thought it was brilliant.

He talks about writing books. 'Shakespeare? J.K. Rowling? Jacqueline Wilson? Biggest liars in the world. All made up, every word.' He goes on like that, trying to shock us. I read some of his stories actually, animal stories, in our proper class, Miss Stani's, and they were quite sad and realistic, not corny like the ones he's been reading now. They gave me the idea he would be quiet and formal, like a vet, maybe a bit sad-looking. But I sure got that wrong, he has turned out to be a nutter.

The Liar stops us all with a massive hurrumph and a glare. She decides to feed him some proper questions to answer and get him back on the subject of the hard and rewarding job of writing.

'Who *inspired* you in your youth?' she booms, hoping he'll say some wonderful teacher like her who made him stay in and learn spellings, he moaned about it then but now he understands...

But there's no way she's going to get that kind of answer from him.

'My old fella,' he says. He tells about the farm in Herefordshire where he grew up, just his father and him. His mother left when he was very small, he remembers he had a mother but can't remember anything about her. He never had any brothers or sisters.

His dad was a bit of a loner who talked to himself a lot. He only cleared up when it was essential, so the author had difficulty finding things he needed for school. His dad wouldn't throw things out either, the place was totally piled up.

'I can't find anything I need for school,' the author said angrily one morning, 'it's too cluttered in here.' When he got home there was a sheep in the kitchen and it stayed there for a week doing droppings and baaing to be let out. Finally he blew up. 'I HATE IT HERE!' he said, 'I can't move because of all the mess.'

'That's alright son,' his dad said, and without another word he opened the door and kicked the sheep back out.

Like I said, a nutter from a long line of nutters, what did I tell you, men are always the wackos, you've only got to watch Blind Date to see that, never mind the crazies in my family, mine and Kim's. But hey, he's coughed up about the tough times he had as a kid, fair play. Sad really. They often are a bit sad in my opinion, men, and you know what? Look in a dictionary for the word crazy. It means broken.

Now what's that about? Mother Nature made a cock-up somewhere? Got it spot-on with us ladies, not with the lads... how can that be right? Maybe it's just they get all the rubbish jobs. I mean destroying kind of jobs, which someone has to do if you want food and airports and all that suchlike. And we get more the creating ones, babies to name one example. It's like earthquakes and storms break things down, and that makes nice fertile fields for the crops to grow. Eventually.

Funny I've done more pages about them though, twice as mad but twice as many pages, so I guess it helps to be a bit crazy or you'd end up like MacAlister, look at her over there all stressed and beaky cause he's not answering the way she wants. Let's face it, a bowl of cat food would be madder than her. And more interesting.

'What about books..?' He's got to say something she can ram down our throats after he's gone, and she's not letting go till he does. He hardly has time to sip his water never mind look for a hand from us kids which he'd much rather answer, it's obvious. 'Did any of the classics inspire you? Tolstoy? Dostoyevski for example?'

'Didn't have many books,' he says straight at her, as if to say, you won't get anywhere trying to manipulate me dear so forget it... 'rats got most of them. I remember the year the lambs were buried in snow-drifts though. Snow, deep... Lambs being born early cause of the mild weather, then a month of snow and freezing temperatures. They were buried in drifts. The old fella made snow-shoes out of wooden boards so we wouldn't sink in, takes a long stick and goes poking in the drifts by the hedges to find them.

He releases the ewes but the lambs are frozen, mostly dead. As he gets to the far corner where the snow's deepest he prods another ewe. A long dig and he reaches it but it won't move. It's in labour. The lamb is stuck, a leg poking out. It's being born the wrong way. He steps into the dip he's dug beside it, kneels down talking quietly to it all the time, and pushes at the leg until it goes back. He pushes it up further, until he can turn it and birth the lamb properly. It bleats in a high voice in the snow. There is blood in the snow. The ewe is yellow against it. My dad's arm is red to the elbow. The new lamb steams and bleats a delicate bleat.

Now that's something I'll never forget.'

As she quietly gags on the thought of the arm up the sheep's thingy and the steaming blood-covered lamb a mass of hands goes up, he's got everyone listening now, they want to know more. Except our moral guide and jailer recovers quick.

'What about your teachers? What did you learn from them that helped you to success in your writing career...?'

He starts as if he's going to give her what she wants at last.

He tells about the village school he went to, where all the kids were in two classes, all ages mixed together. The government was going to close it down, but the parents got placards and said it would be dangerous for their kids to go to the next village in the dark. They were on the news. The government changed its mind.

He had the same teacher all through juniors, Miss Samuels. She had taught his dad as well. She was an institution.

The Liar beams at us. This Miss Samuels sounds promising, a teacher like her, firm but fair, inspiring, gratefully remembered by her pupils the rest of their lives.

'Had hairs growing out of her chin. Grey and curly. Terrifying she was, but she wouldn't ask me when I put my hand up cause she didn't know whether I'd answer the hardest questions right or the easiest ones wrong. But if she ignored me I'd start making farty noises with my book across the table, like this...'

He picks up one of his stories and makes a right rasper across the desk next to him. The hall cracks up, MacAlie trying to throw an invisible net over us with her eyes. He doesn't wait for us to stop, and it's a half a minute before we can all hear again.

'... terrified on my first day of secondary school, getting the same bus as the kids from the estates, laughing and calling me sheep-shagger...'

The play-time bell goes. The Liar shoots up on her feet and gets rid of us. Her ordeal is over. She thinks.

* * *

We laugh some more and then skip out to play, leaving him to get coffee in the staffroom.

'We're not mad enough, that's our trouble,' I yell at the wind when we're out. 'Why should boys have to do all the chaos stuff when we do fields. We ought to help them.' A football comes over, usually I would step out the way to not be charged at by a scrag of them trying to get it, but this time something makes me look at them, all thinking they're Beckham or Giggs, and before

I knew it I'd taken a boot at it and it sailed over the fence.

'Stupid tart,' one of them yells angrily in my face before running over to give his mate a leg-up and keep watch for the teacher.

'Kar-en!' Kim says incredulously. I can't believe what I did either. Feels good inside, kind of powerful and not scared.

'What fields? Talk English. Anyway - we are mad...' Kim's voice back to normal. 'Well, we can be if we want. What about when we put squeezy paint on all the netballs?'

'That was years ago, you can't count what you do in play-school.'

The whistle goes. Benson clings his cold coffee cup to his chest scowling for talkers before letting us back in.

* * *

What happened after the author

It wasn't far off lunch-time. We'd been dumbed down since break with easy maths stuff, not the ideal way to follow up an author's talk. Besides, if you can do it, why go on and on? That's not learning - it's the opposite, cause when your mind goes tired you start making mistakes you wouldn't have before. For some reason I found myself thinking about gramps and the chair - 'I'm entitled to be here, they won't defeat me.' Without looking up I ruled under the last sum and wrote The Liar a message.

'Dear Mrs MacAlister,

This is Karen here, one of the two K. Taylors that seem to get you so confused, I'm the one with the medium brown hair which I tie back in class, the other one with the fair hair and freckles is my cousin Kim. And bigger nose. Kim Taylor? See? Sitting next to me? Not too difficult. Not meaning to be rude, but I really can't stand maths. I can do it standing on my head so it's not cause it's too hard. I prefer technology or science if you might like to know, where you can pick things up and experiment with them. I would just like to say Miss Stanislaus went to a lot of trouble to organise this visit, the least you could do is make a bit of an effort. I'm going to run out of class in a minute and set off the fire-alarm, but by the time you read this all the dramatics will be over and you will probably be at home drinking cocoa in your slippers with darling hubby-wubby.

Nothing personal.

Yours sincerely,
K. Taylor (brown-haired one).'

* * *

The fire-alarm glass was hard to break, I cut the palm of my hand a bit, the round part near the thumb, and realised it wouldn't be so clever to run back in class bleeding which might seem a bit daft considering the note. Besides the bell had started.

The school toilets are disgusting. They smell of stale wee and you can always hear trickling water, makes you feel wet even when you're dry. Hargreaves hates doing them. Even Sophie won't go in and there are lots of tasty soap pieces on the floor.

But the adrenaline was taking over now - I dived in and hid anyway, cross-legged up on a seat, with the door locked, while the whole school emptied itself into the playground. First there were herds of footsteps and teachers' voices, then a few, then a couple running - and silence. Just the trickle of water from the pipes and my heart thumping under my blouse.

What got into me? I had no idea I was going to do any of that stuff. When I woke up it was just another day, not even Friday the thirteenth. But so exciting, I felt like a star.

After a while I calmed down and unfolded my legs. I went out and looked at myself in the wall-mirror opposite and did a triumphant whirl. What next for the world's most daring school havoc-maker?

I decided to do the staffroom and put salt in the sugar and sugar in the salt - and other things, I wasn't sure what. No-one could stop me, the teachers would have to stay outside till the all-clear was given.

* * *

The last few yards down the corridor were quite scary, I could hear my footsteps however lightly I walked, it felt like I would give my position away any moment and Hargreaves would leap out and drag me to the head.

It would just have to be a quick raid on the staffroom, a really quick raid. My heart was thumping so hard I thought it was alive. It is I suppose, in fact you could say the heart is the only part that is alive, if it stops everything else goes belly-up. Anyway, that's enough about that, I put my hand on the door-knob - had to actually restrain myself from knocking politely and waiting. I decided a quick note in MacAlie's tray would do - WE ALL KNOW YOU LIED ABOUT RYAN TAYLOR SO DO THE OTHER TEACHERS. Something like that, just to let her know she hadn't got away with it completely.

The staffroom is an old classroom the council men redecorated - whiteboard is still there with playground rotas on, but everything else is different. Although there are twelve teachers instead of twenty-nine kids, the place is twice as cluttered, the pinboards have two or three layers of notices on top of each other, some hanging off by one pin where the other three have been nicked. Every cup is dirty and standing on the draining-board or lying in a bowl of sloppy water.

There was a single bark as I turned the handle, not Sophie though. Before I could run in terror a wet snout prised it ajar and there was the dog from the stage. I pushed it further, not sure why - to let him out maybe so he wouldn't get trapped in the not-flames. Sitting perfectly relaxed in the chair opposite the door was the author.

'Hello.' Calm voice. 'Sent you to fetch me? Very thoughtful, can't have the author going up in smoke. Don't worry, we're fine here - tell them you saw me go to my car if they ask.'

I couldn't seem to move, he'd completely thrown me being there, and for the first time I came to and realised I'd landed myself in serious trouble.

He must have realised too - that's writer's intuition for you - realised they couldn't possibly send a kid back in to check I suppose, then he just seemed to make the connection.

'You know how to make a statement alright. What were you trying to say..? Gip, here...'

His dog stopped sniffing my legs and ambled back to him with a swish of the tail.

'What do you mean, say?'

'Well - what did you want to tell them? They're all lined up waiting. Has someone upset you?'

'Maybe.'

'Teacher?' He raised an eyebrow.

'That one.' I pointed to her tray, it was in the middle row, at least I think it was, depends if the names went above or below. A brief image of my hate-note going in the wrong teacher's tray passed through my mind. Actually that wouldn't be a bad idea. 'She was the one in the hall.'

He raised an eyebrow slightly. His eyes were deep, they went with his voice.

'Was it bad?'

'Very.' I told him. Everything. My statement. It was quite refreshing in a way, the whole school outside in lines like a jury and him like a judge listening to the evidence. Just needed her in the accused box. 'Do you swear to tell the truth, the whole truth and nothing but the truth SO HELP YOU GOD..'

God. I wish.

'Hmm...' he says when I finish, 'so she gets away scott free and you dig a damn great hole for yourself.'

'Cheek...' I leave the sentence hanging, I was sure I knew how to finish it when I thought it. I mean, I've done quite a daring thing for a kid, and that's the best he can say.

'I've done quite a daring thing for a kid...' It tails away as if the wind's dropped.

'Very daring,' he says. 'Charge of the Light Brigade. "C'est magnifique, mais ce n'est pas la guerre..." Magnificent, but a dumb way to fight. Roughly.'

Who's he calling dumb? I take a breath, might as well go the whole hog now I've got this far.

'You know - not meaning to be rude, but why d'you write children's stories? Haven't you sort of got the courage to do ones for adults yet?'

He thinks it over. I'm not that interested really, just want to get him back.

'No, I'm not sure I have. Still trying to get to the truth of my childhood I guess.'

'That's clever, we're all trying like stink to get away from being kids and grow up, and you're trying to go back there. I mean, don't take this personally, but maybe that's why some of your stories are sort of, boring... If you're going the wrong way I mean. Anyway - why do stories in the first place if you're looking for the truth? That should be non-fiction shouldn't it? Fact: non-fiction - Made-up: fiction. You learn that in infants.'

He sips his coffee. He's strange alright, you can't ruffle him. But I think I like him really, or might if I got to know him, it's the ones you can wind up whenever you feel like I hate.

'I've been thinking more and more it might be the other way round. Kids ask the same questions everywhere I go - where do you get your ideas, what's your favourite book... I answer as truthfully as I can, but my answers change. So there must be a lot of truths, not just one. When I say I write to get to the truth of my childhood, I mean I make up different stories to try out different truths. I only know how true they are when they're done. If I recognise them, I guess that means I've found one of the truths I was looking for.'

'It rings true...' It jumps out of my mouth, don't ask me why.

'Exactly. Trouble is, I don't know how many others there are - could be infinite.'

He is seriously weird.

'You're quite weird you know,' I say, putting my hand out to his dog to show I'm not deliberately offending still. But my words seem to boom in the emptiness and don't feel quite right. I mean there are his animal stories for one thing, they ring true. Just cause he didn't choose to read them out... Then I remember.

'O.K., that's fiction, just say fiction doesn't always mean untrue for a minute. What about the other half? Fact: non-fiction. You can't say facts aren't true can you, facts are facts. Full-stop.'

He breathes into his coffee without drinking it. Maybe it feeds his thoughts, or warms them.

'Well, try this: you've set off the alarm to annoy your teacher. To express your annoyance. Fact? Fact. You say that's not a statement, but I say it is. Your statement is, "I'm a girl Bin Laden and I'm going to show my friends and brothers we can be strong. We may not have as much power as them but we can attack their systems." That means you've made yourself up as a character - you've turned your fact into fiction.'

Well that's typical of an author, going on about anything that comes into his head.

'You can't call me Bin Laden. No way...'

'Forget Bin Laden. When you punched the fire-bell glass you were doing hero of the underdogs, vengeance for your cousin and brother maybe. You were doing a story, not real life. It's O.K. - good luck with the fire-alarm thing, but don't do the avenging hero too long, they get hunted down. You need to get real again. Quick...'

Cripes he's right, they're coming in. The dog's up yipping a greeting. I panic for the first time.

He's on his feet.

'Where's the sick-bay?'

'Eh..?' I haven't got time for him now.

'Medical room. Have you got one?'

'Ah... down the corridor, couple of doors.'

I prepare to dash for it, not sure where, toilets again I suppose. What's up with him anyway...

'Nip in there and lie down. Look ill. I'll say I found you vomiting or something. Go on... And remember, keep your apples and pears apart.'

'You what?'

'Facts and fictions. Don't mix them up. Bye... Go.'

Jesus. I dive for the M.I. couch and try to make my head spin. I wanted to say something wise back, not just go. If it was wise that is, which I doubt. But there was no time. Ah well, great saboteur and literary thinker becomes dipsy fibby schoolgirl again. Fact.

Mrs Davies the sec. flings open the door and heaves a gasp of relief. They're so glad they've located me they don't even consider the ill bit. Being as there wasn't a fire in the first place I can only assume they're relieved they can finish the lines of ticks on the registers.

* * *

Tues 11th of November (Poppy Day)

'You BITCH!!'

Leanne shouts right out in the middle of class. The Liar jumps up and grabs her arm and takes her to the front.

'How dare you girl,' she says, face deep red with anger, 'that might be how you behaved in your old class, but it's not how to behave in my class.'

She doesn't waste much time getting in her stride, MacAlie. Some teachers can't function till they've had a couple of cups of coffee first thing, but in her case it takes a damn good rant to start her up. I wouldn't mind but it's only about a pen.

'But miss, she...'

'NO BUTS! You deliberately shouted out.'

'But she...'

'DID YOU HEAR ME? You're not listening.'

'She bust my pen miss.'

'I don't care if she broke into the Bank of England and stole a truck-load of gold bullion - you do not SHOUT in my classroom. DO YOU HEAR?'

'It was new miss.'

'I don't care if it was hand-crafted from silver and emeralds by a master craftsman, I will NOT have you shouting in my class. Now that's enough, I don't want to hear any more.'

'It cost two pound ninety-nine miss.'

'I DON'T CARE if it cost half-the-winnings-of-the-National-Lottery and ninety-nine p, THERE WILL BE NO SHOUTING IN MY ROOM, IS THAT CLEAR?'

'She took it without asking.'

'I don't care if she kidnapped an old lady, shut her in a cellar, chopped her up in tiny pieces and fed her to the seagulls, I WON'T have you shouting and yelling in my classroom.'

'Sorry miss.'

'I DON'T CARE if you get down on your hands and knees and offer to... pardon?'

'Sorry miss.'

'Er, yes, well, I should think so... Broke your pen you say?'

'Yes miss - but it's alright, it doesn't really matter.'

'OH DOESN'T IT... We'll see about that. TRACEY MARCHANT - COME OUT HERE. I'd like a quiet word with you.'

It's amazing how something you heard and ignored can come back and smack you right between the eyes. I've just sat back to enjoy MacAlie's pre-lesson entertainment, I mean you can't take her seriously you really can't, when I realise with an unbelievable flash the author chap was right. She's in a fiction role the whole time. She's not Jenny MacAlister or whatever her name is teaching in a primary school for a living, no way. She's the queen of family values holding back hoards of foul-mouthed little ruffians until we learn enough manners to sit at the adult table. That's how she sees herself. And us.

Miss Stanislaus is an example of an ordinary woman who's got a life and does teaching for her job, that's why she has a laugh with the other teachers, they play jokes on each other and enjoy themselves. For example one of the teachers last year was a man who had a habit of slipping out of class while the kids were working to get a fresh coffee, and Miss Stanislaus who everyone thought fancied him, maybe she did, sneaked in and got all the kids to leave their work and hide in the P.E. store, and when he came into her scratching his head she acted innocent. He took ten minutes to find them and then it was only cause one of them laughed.

I'll tell you who The Liar really is. She's the leader of the world crusade against evil, and the more she lobs her bombs at us the more little Bin Ladens she makes. He was dead right, the author bloke, she's got her apples and pears totally mixed up, and that means she can never be at peace. The poor poor cow.

* * *

Sat 15th Nov

Gramps is in the first stages of Parkinsons. Luckily he moved in before they realised; if he had moved in after they would have treated him as if he were helpless, like a child, a sad old child - but he had a couple of years there first and they got to know him.

Even so, he was standing at the war memorial at eleven o'clock last Tuesday, in silence probably at exactly the time MacAlie was shelling our lines with her ranting, now he's trying to shock me with one of his war stories. He thinks I don't know he's doing the wrong war, he couldn't possibly have been in the first one he wouldn't have been born. I also know he wasn't in the last one, the Hitler one - well, he was I suppose, but only as a boy. Dad told me about his mum taking them down to hide in the coal cellar when the sirens went off.

Maybe he tells the stories cause he felt helpless. Sixty-odd years is a long time to go on feeling helpless mind.

'They shot a boy so many times his head fell away; the headless body hung from the wire, and two more got shot trying to fetch it back. He would have been seventeen probably, eighteen, his parents reading their telegram from the War Ministry thinking at least he died a hero. Not knowing they were having a sweepstake to see who could blow the last visible part of his head away.

That's why I'd have volunteered as a sewer rat, a tunneller, digging right under the enemy trenches to lay explosives. Not so easy to get shot in a tunnel.

Mind, the tunnels did collapse sometimes and bury them alive. And if the Germans happened to be digging from the other way they'd tunnel right in to each other, then there'd be bayonet fights in the pitch dark, cause the lamps went out as soon as they heard. They durstn't fire guns, the bullets'd ricochet off and end up in their own chests. But I'd still have joined the sewer rats rather than face the bullets and barbed wire above. How about you...?'

He sits back feeling pleased with himself. It's like one of those things where you say what would you rather die of, heat or cold? He waits for me to squirm with indecision, but I just look straight at him and say, 'I think you've got your apples and pears mixed up there gramps,' and smile.

A funny thing happens on the way out. I hear a pop-song I vaguely know being sung to some backing music behind a door. It says Staff. I hover about and listen for a minute, it's quite good. One of the supervisors scurries past to deal with something.

'That's Emma doing her Stars in Their Eyes thing, good isn't she..'

The door opens. A quizzical face looks out, quite long and gaunt with a glossy wig of jet black straight hair.

'Wanna listen?' she says, having established I'm not dangerous. I shrug my shoulders and slip in for a minute, there's a chair by the door. It turns out she works mostly night shifts, the ones people don't want to do, so she can practise. Fairly quietly. She has a driving ambition to be Cher, and intends to enter Stars in their Eyes when she's ready. She'll surprise everyone apart from the other members of staff who obviously know all about it and don't mind her skiving to practise. But not yet. Only when she's ready.

I tell her I think she's nearly ready now, and get away. Actually she wouldn't win it but she might just get on if she's lucky. I have the feeling the real reason she's putting it off is she doesn't want her dream to be spoiled. Her fiction. Still, at least she's up front about it, not like some people.

* * *

Monday 17th November

A new girl has come into the class, transferred from private school. Kim recognises her, she's got her own pony and it's stabled down the yard where Kim mucks out on Saturday mornings for free rides. She doesn't recognise Kim though, much to Kim's aggrievance if there is such a word. If you come from private school to ordinary school there's a very delicate transfer process, cause they have to prove they're worthy of us rough ones' company first before we'll accept them. But of course The Liar blunders straight in and gets her to tell us all about herself and her family so we can look up to her as a role-model of good values, and the poor cow has no choice but to do it.

She has one sister who is seventeen and goes to performing arts college and a little brother who's away at prep-school. So Heidi is almost the only child now oh tush tush. Sometimes her sis comes home for a couple of days to learn lines for the plays they do at college and gets her to help, by following the script and prompting her when she goes wrong. She tells all this in an over-correct phoney voice so it sounds false, as if it's lines in a play she's rehearsing not her crummy sister and we're the drones forced to listen and prompt politely if she goes wrong. Her fiction, AAYAH... everyone's at it, I'm going to go mad. She has her own bedroom with Westlife pictures and a cat called Moggy.

Kim hates her already. We're in the toilets at break and she's in one of the cubicles.

'Is she still in there?'

'Think so.'

'She gets tons of lessons but she still can't ride properly, her rosettes are all purple and brown.'

'Isn't that good? It sounds O.K.'

'GOOD? It's the lowest you can get, they give them to tiddlies for getting on and off properly. You know what she did last weekend?'

'Shh - she can hear.'

'I'll turn a tap on. There - she said she was mucking out but she never. His straw looked clean but that was only the top, she just spread some over. Underneath it was still solid thingy - manure.'

'Eugh, poor thing, he'll be treading in it all day won't he?'

'That's why he looks so mangy. Cow. Let's chuck water over the door, ready? One, two, three!'

'HEY, WHO DID THAT? I'LL TELL...'

'Ooops, sorry, wrong one. Quick, scarper...'

*   *   *

I think Kim is getting back to her old self again. Being as MacAlie is the outright champion moaner of all teachers, she changed the date from Monday to Moanday. MacAlie notices after play and gets cross, not because it was rude - she doesn't even know she's a moaner, thinks she's the friend and protector of all children actually - but cause she really thought someone couldn't spell Monday.

'Come on, own up - who can't spell the days of the week?' Silence. '*Moanday*... my goodness - I suppose whoever it is would write Tuesday: *Chooseday*.'

We snorted with giggles at our desks and she gently told us to calm down. Thought we'd gone into hysterics at her wit. That made us giggle even harder.

'I said, ENOUGH...' she snapped at last, but you could still tell how flattered she was. In the end we managed to stop, but by that time the kids who weren't laughing before had joined in. They knew how to work it.

She kept us in for ten minutes at lunch, so in P.E. we got manic and she made us get changed early. So we got some wet soap and rammed it in the keyhole of her office so she couldn't get the key in. She gave the whole class a detention and we had to take a form home to our parents and get it signed to say they knew we were being kept in after school. That's the first time that's ever happened to me.

So congratulations MacAlister, in less than a month you've proved it once again, like you do every year - only this year twice - that all kids are the same and can't be trusted an inch. I've got just one thing to say to you: it's all fiction, and the only one who's been taken in is you. I feel like writing a letter to my author friend and telling him he's not so weird after all. How do you do that? Just send it to Scholastic Books London I suppose. Miss would probably know, though it would be a bit rich asking her where I should post the biggest slagging she's ever had to.

* * *

Weds 26th November

Looks like me and Kim aren't the only ones doing Bin Laden round here - Ry has allowed Baldy a generous three weeks to get used to him, now he's giving him the treatment. Mind, Ry isn't exactly new to terrorism, he got into his stride when he was about three.

He's developed an interest in the occupants of Baldy's aquarium for starters.

'Look me in the eye Taylor.'

'Sir.'

'Look me in the eye when you talk to me.'

'I am sir.'

'No. No you're not, your eyes are all over the place. You haven't looked at the same place for more than two seconds. What's the matter, guilty conscience?'

'No sir.'

'Well tell me why you keep looking at your feet. Is there something down there boy? What are you looking at?'

'Nothing sir.'

'Where are you boy? Not in the present world that's for sure. I can't get a sane answer from you.'

'Don't know sir. Aah. Let me go sir.'

'Now then, say you're sorry.'

'Sir, you're hurting my ear.'

'What's the little word...'

'I never done anything.'

'I saw you boy.'

'It was Steven.'

'He was outside. You were the only one in the classroom.'

'My ear sir, you're not allowed to - '

'And you're not allowed to pour my tea in the fish tank, are you? Look at them.'

'Sir they're still swimming.'

'They're slowly dying Taylor, because of you.'

'I didn't mean it sir.'

'You did it accidentally...'

'Sir.'

'You picked up the cup accidentally, right?'

'I thought it was empty.'

'It is. You emptied it.'

'I'll clean them out sir.'

'I know. Now say sorry.'

'Sorry.'

'Sorry, what?'

'My ear sir...'

'No. Not sorry my ear. Sorry what?'

'I'm telling my dad...'

'Are you now. He'll enjoy that. Sorry, what?'

'Sorry sir.'

'Better. Now say it to the fish.'

'Sir?'

'The fish - not me - they're the ones you've poisoned.'

'Sir..'

'The fish.'

'Sorry fish.'

'They didn't hear you...'

'... SORRY FISH.'

'Now empty the tank and clean them out before I make you drink it.'

Actually, Baldy should be flattered - Ry hadn't been in trouble for at least a fortnight, Aunt Rache was beginning to worry. But you can tell he's getting his confidence back now.

* * *

Thurs 27th November

Not that I'm sympathetic, but it's quite bad luck for the new girl walking straight into the middle of a small battlefield and being recruited for the wrong side. I mean if The Liar tells her she's been appointed as book monitor she can't exactly say stick it can she. She trudges up the rows handing us our books with every tiny mistake underlined and it's difficult not to get the feeling she's the one who marked them as well.

Another thing: MacAlie's on the stars trail. We're all doing our best not to get any cause it's insulting to people of our age, on the thresh-hold of our life-changing leap into high school-ness. Miss Stanislaus would never have diminished us like that, she doesn't even do them that seriously with her new tiddlies. But poor old Heidi keeps being given jobs, then getting hundreds of stars dumped in her lap. She could start up a new chart of her own at this rate she'd still get more than the rest of us added together. If MacAlie had a brain in her head she'd realise the kindest thing she could do would be to kick her out in the cold with everyone else and tell her to get on with it. Or make her stay in and practise thumping a punch-bag all break. But instead she gives her jobs, and now she's started doing them without being asked, cause she knows no-one likes her and would rather be indoors. She's collecting stars by the kilo.

She's also managed to walk straight into the main part in the nativity.

'Listen to her, show-off, can't act for a toffee: "I shall name the baby Jesus and he shall be a prophet to all mankind..", hope she wets herself.... Anyway, something'll happen soon, you wait and see.'

'What d'you mean?'

'There's going to be a little accident right in the middle of Mary blinkin Magdelene's main speech.'

'What little accident?'

'Hmm... you'll know when it happens.'

'Come on Kim, tell...'

'Can't, I promised not to.'

'I'll mess your hair up.'

'O.K. O.K. keep your kegs on.. Michael Duggan's going to knock the tin of frankincense off the table when she's speaking and make it look like an accident.'

'God, it won't half clatter, we dropped it before, remember, getting it out of the box.'

'Yeh I know, should mess her up real good - bit of luck she'll muck up the rest of her lines.'

'Cool.'

* * *

Saturday 29th November

Gramps is always with it even when he seems to be out of it. I've been telling him about MacAlie (again) but he's gradually closed his eyes and let me drone on. There's silence for a bit after I stop, he seems very tired today, and gradually I tune in to a conversation next to us. It's a couple of old biddies talking about someone who's died.

‘Well, he had a good life... ‘

‘He was a dirty old man, good riddance to him.’

‘Maureen, you can’t talk like that, we were all at the funeral.’

‘I don’t care if we were. May the Lord strike me down if I tell a lie...‘

‘You mustn’t speak ill off the dead over a bit of dirt, a bit of dirt never hurt anyone.’

‘I’m not talking about that kind of dirt. I saw him looking at the magazines in Smiths.’

‘You’re allowed to do that Maureen. I look at the gardening mags. Never buy one, they’re far too expensive, you could hire a gardener for the price. I just check to see what they’re recommending and put them back.’

‘Not these ones you wouldn’t... They’re wrapped in plastic for a start. Disgusting I call them, ought to be pulped. He used to go in there and get one of the assistants to fetch them down off the shelf for him.’

‘He never did..’

‘May the Lord strike me down if I tell a lie. Then he’d pull the wrapper open under their noses and start flicking through the pages. Bold as you please.’

‘Well, I thought he was a gentleman. He used to help in the church hall when he was fit, and never ask a penny for his trouble.’

‘No - he was probably taking it out of the collection box, that’s why.’

'Maureen! May the Lord strike you down if you tell a lie... '

Without opening his eyes gramps suddenly says, 'Blimey she's vanished - what's that funny burning smell?'

* * *

Mon December the 1st

'What's Santa going to put in your stocking Kim?'

'Don't get stockings, just tell em to give me money instead... You know what he did the last year he lived with us..?'

'Who, Uncle Don?'

'Dad, yeh. Got drunk - really drunk - then when he crept in with the presents he crashed through the door and fell on them.'

'Wow, poor you. D'he bust any?'

'Yeh, his leg. Spent Christmas Day in hospital having it put in plaster.'

I remember that Christmas. He always figured his job was to do the stockings and Aunt Rache's was to prepare the dinner, so he came staggering back at midnight and crept up to the bedrooms. Well, he thought he was creeping. Ry had left his scooter by the door so Santa could use it to get back to his sleigh quickly, and Uncle Don fell over it, wacked his leg on the bunk ladder and broke them both - ladder and leg. Ry got down pretty quick without the ladder anyway.

In the end they had a nice quiet Christmas without him. Didn't stop him getting drunk again on New Year's Eve though. You could say he was plastered all over Christmas.

*　　　*　　　*

Friday 5th Dec

They are doing end-of-term trips, you had to sign lists in the hall for the one you wanted. Ice-skating had ninety-seven signatures squashed in all over the list, up the sides and everywhere, the museum trip had two. Underneath in felt pen someone scrawled 'DUMB TRIP' but they either didn't notice or decided it wasn't worth the hassle. But they've managed to con some of the younger ones to go by telling them there are skeletons. Also anyone in the nativity so they can be back in time for rehearsals. Plus us...

Most of Shaun's year are there, having the time of their lives.

'... Come on lads, in here, it's all coins.'

'Hang on, I'm drawing this spider for my worksheet...'

'Spider? There's no spiders in here, it's bones.'

'Not in the cases dope, underneath - look, there.'

'URGH, it's alive! Squash the bugger.'

'Hoy, you've disturbed it now.'

'Who cares. We've found gold coins...'

'Wow, hey look at that shiny one, looks like it's just been minted. Ry, you're the smallest, lean over and read the date on it.'

'Give us a leg up then... Seventeen... Ah, what was that?'

'Get down! You've cracked the glass.'

'Come on scarper quick. What's that bell..?'

'Alarm. You've set off the bloody burglar alarm. Quick, in here - Tudor Fashion, pretend we're doing the questionnaires.'

*   *   *

We're just wandering through the rooms chilling.

'Look at old Benson staring at that statue of the lady with the bosum coming out of her dress.'

'Yeh, turning his head sideways like an expert.'

'He's taking a long time isn't he?'

'Yeh, come on, let's go to Maccy D's and see if there's anything.'

'Yeh, who cares about boobs... Just going toilet sir.'

'Yeh, sorry to spoil your concentration sir.'

We giggle off out. It's only a couple of doors down - and surprise surprise, the first person we see is queen of the stars, Mary Magdelene. She's sneaked off for a McFlurry, the little devil.

As we make our way to the counter, a stunning awareness comes to me. I knew I'd seen her somewhere. It was here, with her little brother and her dad. I suddenly feel unbelievable sadness for her, and have to stop myself going over and begging forgiveness for all the mean things we've done. Not that Kim would let me if she knew. I tell her what I've just realised. She says she can't remember the time in McDonald's even though she's seen her loads since at the yard. I say I'm going to talk to her, and when she sees I mean it she flounces out. Heidi has noticed.

'My friend knows you from your horse-yard place...'

'I know she does. So...'

'Sorry we've been so mean, honest, it's just MacAlie really...' I should have said that first. She's still waiting to see if there's a catch. 'Actually I know you from before as well, kind of - I was in here when your dad was trying to get them to make him some peculiar tea...'

I squinch my nose up to show I'm on-side, and suddenly the gates open.

'Earl Grey, don't remind me. He's so embarrassing. Or was, we don't see much of him now...'

We settle down to a good old anti-dad gossip. Her mum is a beautician and her dad is in finance and works abroad quite a bit which is why they don't see much of him, that, and because they don't really want to and their mum doesn't want them to either. Her pony is called Cherokee. It was a kind of sop when they took her out of private school cause her dad couldn't afford to send her brother to prep as well and his education is his little project. Probably why she doesn't look after it very well, if it reminds her of being taken away from her friends and put with us common lot. I crinkle my face.

'Poor you, it must have been horrible...'

'What, leaving the cathedral school, you're joking, you have to sit in your blazers all day and kids chuck their crisp bags at you on the bus. I just don't know why they had to go and get a pony cause of one little thing I said when I was about six. Think of the holidays we could have had...'

Holidays are something I know about having recently got back from a less than perfect example. We swap stories.

'I'll tell you the worst one we ever had.' She hasn't realised it but she's at last beginning to sound like one of us... 'Shanklin, Isle of Wight. It was after he left - I think he came back, maybe they were giving it another try. Anyway he wanted to take us all on holiday...

"I've always wanted to see the Needles," he says, "don't know why, just have."

"Needles?" I say, "What Needles? What are they?"

I guess it must be a science park with lots of dials and ammeters and things.

"Very pretty chalk formations that stick out of the sea. Like gigantic teeth."

"Chalk formations? Are they building something then?"

"No-one's building anything, they're just natural, built by Mother Nature, if you like..."

"Just scenery, you mean..." I say, "What about democracy then?" Our family used to vote on holidays.

"Too far - and they don't speak English."

He's about as funny as Les Dennis.

So we ended up at dad's famous Needles. He blabbed on about achieving a little dream from boyhood then a couple of days later he wasn't there any more, he'd got bored and gone - end of holiday, end of the new beginning.'

She's quite nice when she stops doing the teacher's stooge thing - if people want to like you they'll like you, even teachers, it's their choice not yours. Once she realises The Liar simply doesn't count anyway she'll be fine. I think we might be able to help a bit there.

Next thing a small whirlwind comes through the door and stops next to us. My side.

'They're looking for you, come on, we're all lined up ready.'

We both get up. Kim's only addressed me, but I include Heidi. I ought to warn her that if we're going to be friends she'd better prepare herself for some serious jealousy, but I don't want to complicate her life more than it already is. Anyway, Kim should know by now she'll always come first.

* * *

Mon 8th Dec

But things come to a head before I predicted. She's given out invites to her birthday party, which is a big mistake. Next year maybe, but not this.

There are whispered discussions round school whether to all boycott it or go and mess it up. I try to tell

Kim some of the things she's said to me so she'll understand a bit but she's determined not to let the facts spoil her fun.

'Huh, I wouldn't mind a mum who gives me all the money I want.'

'She doesn't, not any more, they aren't rich now. Very. And she has to stay in all the time in case she starts hanging round with the wrong sort.'

'Huh, she doesn't hang round with anyone. Too snotty.'

'Yeh, but her mum thinks she would if she got the chance.'

'Like who?'

'Us, for example.'

'Flippin nerve...'

'Only joking..'

*   *   *

Sat 13th of December

It's no good, takes more than a few weak jokes to neutralise pure hate. I ought to pull Kim's hair out really, but end up meekly going along and hoping they'll change their minds about her once they get there.

Fat chance. There are hoity-toities from her old school as well.

'O.K. everyone - Chinese Whispers... Ready?'

'Boring...'

'Shh, she'll hear you.'

'So...'

'Hermione can be first...'

Some of the other girls jump on their toes and clap, Hermione's obviously their champion.

'Eu Hermarnie.'

'Don't Kim, it's her party, do what she wants.'

'Don't have to.'

'Come on, it's only Chinese Whispers.'

'I'm gonna spoil it.'

'Don't Kim, you can't...'

'Try me.'

'Shhh, they're starting.'

'My mum's got a pair of posh pyjamas.'

'My mum's got a pair of posh pyjamas.'

'My mum's wearing posh pyjamas.'

'My mum's wearing posh pyjamas.'

'My mum's wearing posh pyjamas.'

You can hear anyway. Kim sneers as it makes its way round.

'I've got a bum like a squashed banana.'

'I never said that...'

'Tough, that's what it came round as so you've got to say it.'

'Say what? Oh come on Heidi, we never heard...'

'Bitch.'

A massive fight breaks out between them, they circle slowly round clutching handfuls of each other's hair, shrieking but not daring to be the first to let go.

One of her daft friends from the other school goes into hysterics.

'Throw water on them. Throw water. That's what we have to do with the hounds.'

Next thing a jug of orange squash sloshes over the pair of them and they stop dead, panting fiercely as if shipwrecked. Her mum comes in and the party abruptly ends.

She's invited too many kids who didn't really like her, and mixed them with her friends from the other place. I knew she shouldn't have but didn't know her well enough to stop her. Probably thought we'd all unite in liking her in the end as it was a lavish party, but it's gone the other way. The ones in my class have proved to themselves she's a posh cow, which they only thought before, and the others have proved she's gone down to live among the lower class oiks which they only suspected before.

* * *

Monday the 15th Dec

Very bad news. I've been suspended for a week - last week of term. Me. Karen Taylor.

Quite clever how it happened, what with the commotion of Heidi starting in our form and things I forgot to sneak my book from the pile on MacAlie's desk and rip out the page with the note about the fire-alarm. I signed my own death warrant and left it for her to find.

Graham hovers feebly in the back-ground while mum clutches the letter from school and hyper-ventilates, half of me wants to laugh he looks so uncomfortable, as if he was my partner in crime when I did it but daresn't own up. She's got an appointment to discuss the disturbing lapse in my behaviour.

BUT.

But but but but but oh god oh god... She can't go, gramps has had a stroke, we have to dash to the hospital.

Shaun plays up and wants to go to school, he likes it now. Anyway it's P.E.

While mum is rushing round trying to think of things, Graham senses he is being summoned to rise to the awesome duty of stand-in father. He crouches to Shaun's level, big mistake.

'Now we're going to visit gramps. You mustn't be shocked if he looks a little different...'

'What d'you mean different?'

'Well, er, not quite so healthy-looking as we - you remember... and maybe there will be some tubes in his arms and possibly one in his nose.'

'I don't want to go.'

'Well it would be nice if we all went.'

'It won't be nice for me. I don't want to see him with tubes. What are they for?'

'Well, he may not have them.. but if he does, they sort of feed him and er - sometimes replace the blood.'

'Why?'

'Well it... to help make him better.'

'Is it bad then?'

'No it's not bad, it's very good, good for gramps's body.'

'Is he dying then?'

'Er, um... Christine..'

'Of course not darling. But you mustn't say anything. Do you understand. We don't want to upset him in case he gets worse.'

'That means you think he is. Why can't anyone say anything?'

'Don't be silly darling, you wouldn't want to tell someone they're dying, there'd be tears and all sorts. He's not anyway, I don't know what you were thinking about.'

'Maybe he'd like to know. Maybe he'd like to think about it a bit and be sure he's ready.'

'That's enough. Go and do your teeth and get in the car.'

I'm dead in my heart. I can't feel anything at all, only think.

* * *

When we get there he looks at the ceiling, not us. There are tubes like Graham said and a monitor. Shaun cries and squirms to go, as if gramps isn't really there and doesn't have to be considered. Which he isn't, not Shaun's gramps anyway, the one he knows. Mum takes him into the corridor to calm down.

Graham soundlessly moves his chair back a bit, and without looking away from gramps I check something out about him. He cares. He's moved back a respectful distance, but stayed in when it would have been easier to go out with the others. Just in case.

Gramps's skin is paper already, I feel every bone in his hand. It clutches back. I hold tight tight with my warm little fleshy girl's hand, I've got life to spare, if I could only give some to him, like a transfusion like a transfusion of life if I could just give him some of mine. I can spare it. I would so much like to give him life.

His eyes painfully turn a few degrees in their sockets and attach themselves to mine, they have an unbearable depth, I know they have seen things only dying eyes are allowed to see. Slow slow messages to his brain register me, and at last they seem to come to rest. We look unflinching for a long time, it is not awkward, there is a highway between us like a stretch of open track running to tunnels at each end.

When he has fully absorbed me I speak. My mouth speaks.

'Are you dying gramps?'

It goes down the track, disappears in the tunnel and stops at a station underground. Somewhere in his face a signal changes from amber to green. That is his answer.

'Are you afraid?'

Another wait. The signal goes to amber. I watch a long time. The embankment becomes gramps' face again, and my watching floods with love and sadness.

I let my breathing steady. Another thought leaves my station, I can feel the vibrations. Last one, timetable suspended. I have just managed to board it in time.

'Gramps... is God an apple or a pear?'

Another wait, but no signal. Then his lips move for the first time, but no word comes. We've gone past his station. In a panic I call to him.

'You can't just... Where will you go?'

But the door swings open, a nurse swishes round to the other side of his bed and starts tucking and patting as if he's an item displayed on a market stand.

'He needs his rest I'm afraid.'

My eyes break contact for the first time, but my hand is still in touch, I'd forgotten. There is the slightest change of pressure, a squeeze almost, then he releases his grip and lets me go.

* * *

Outside, Shaun can't wait to get away. He grabs Graham and tugs him towards the stairs. 'That's the way,' says Graham establishing a rhythm with him, 'down the apples and pears...'

He turns and with a face full of sympathy catches my eye for a second.

* * *

Tuesday 30th December.

I was looking forward to Christmas but in the end there wasn't one, really, because of gramps.

* * *

There are two letters I have to write, one voluntary, one compulsory. I do the voluntary one first. It's to the author, I'm quite proud of being suspended in a way and I write to brag about it and tell him he was right, they did hunt me down, but it's O.K. they've only suspended me, not executed. I also apologise for calling his books boring, which is not totally honest as I still feel the same about them, some anyway. And also to tell him I'm thinking of writing a book and would like to know if he could give me some advice. This is another thing not quite true - I mean I would like to write a book, yes, if it would kind of write itself while I held the pen, but I don't really intend to, not this exact moment in time anyway. I think I'm really writing to let him know his disciple's doing fine and keeping up the good work in his absence, that's all.

The other is to The Liar. I have to show remorse and humility as a condition of coming back.

'Dear Mrs MacAlister,

I would like to take this opportunity to apologise for all the trouble and unnecessary irritation my behaviour caused you, and I realise the school had no alternative but to punish me.

My thoughtless action distracted the other pupils of the school and prevented them from continuing the curriculum, not to mention the inconvenience and stress to the staff and Mr Hargreaves who probably had to deal with the damage resulting from my actions.

Not only did I do an unacceptable thing, but also caused you extra work in your own time when you could have had some refreshment and a chance to unwind after your efforts on our behalf by lying about it to try and avoid punishment.

Lying about something you have done so as not to get blamed is one of the worst things anyone can do in life, especially if you are prepared to let someone else get in trouble for it, someone younger for example who can't defend themselves easily. If a person no matter who they are or what age does a thing like that they might think they have got away with it but they have to live with themselves afterwards.

But even though I had the honesty to own up - Miss - I know what I did was a disgraceful thing to admit and a fact I am deeply ashamed of, and you have my word I will not do it or anything like it again.

Yours truly,
Karen Taylor.'

* * *

Monday 5th Jan - new term.

I'm admitted I won't exactly say lovingly back into school after my week of porridge at the end of last term. To my astonishment Heidi is now a senior member of Kim's posse. Now what the heck's that all about? Kim either can't figure it out herself or can't be bothered to tell me, it's like I'm someone who's fallen behind. Probably impressed she could look after herself in the fight or something. Anyway, Heidi's passed her initiation rite by bringing in one of her dad's Meatloaf albums and sneaking it in the school assembly system the day before the end of term so instead of Elgar's Cello Concerto they get Bat Out of Hell full volume when the head switches it on. Obviously she loses the C.D., you couldn't exactly ask for it back could you, but she's not bothered. Her old lady was probably glad to see the back of it.

Just to reaffirm her leadership, Kim hid in the dress-up cupboard before assembly the next day (last day), put a complete bear costume on, then when the head got everyone quiet she sprang out and roared through the rows and out the back. By the time everyone had recovered she was gone - hiding in another cupboard taking it off. In the chaos she sneaked back in her ordinary clothes and never got caught.

Looks like I missed a few decent days.

But that's not all. Although my adventure with the fire-alarm has made me a minor folk-hero in the mischief roll of honour, Kim makes it clear there is work to be done to maintain my reputation. Heidi has managed to get three 'Scream' outfits from a hallowe'en party they had at her other school and the plan is to hide after lessons and spook The Liar while she's quietly marking books.

I take a deep breath. It's not just that if I got caught again they'd put me down as a serious delinquent and I'd get refused for colleges and stuff later on, never mind have to see an education psychologist. It's also I don't want to be Bin Laden any more, MacAlie's not really worth it.

I make a compromise. This is the last thing. One last thing for what she did to Ryan, though he couldn't give a monkey's any more, it got him a better teacher. We agree on a time and a rendezvous.

One final, serious piece of news whilst I was serving my sentence, about Miss Stanislaus. Kim tells in her own special way.

'Hoy Kaz, guess what I heard in the sec's office..'

'What were you doing there?'

'Late book. Guess what they were saying...'

'Dunno - how many for dinners?'

'Nope. Better, tons better. About Miss Stanislaus. Don't tell anyone, right?'

'O.K., spill then.'

'She's having a b-a-b-y...'

'BABY?! WOW... She's not married though, they might have to sack her...'

'I only heard, I'm not sure...'

'Yeh you are. It could get in the papers - "UNMARRIED TEACHER ADMITS PREGNANCY". They do print that kind of thing.'

'Yeh - what can we do?'

'Nothing, just keep quiet and wait I suppose.'

'Yeh.'

* * *

{I'll tell you what Kim actually heard if you like, though we didn't find out till a couple of months later when they announced it. An even more deadly bit of gossip, she just didn't realise: Miss was applying for jobs in other schools. Now you can see why The Liar ought to be strung up can't you, it affects all sorts of people when you do what she did, not just the ones you first thought. Miss - Miss Stanislaus - was telling them in the office, and the secretary was asking her what she thought her chances of being chosen were, as she is still quite young. She started to say she was expecting to at least get an interview, but only got as far as 'I'm expecting..' when she realised Kim had come in, so she stopped herself.}

* * *

Tuesday 6th Jan.

I'm going through the hall at lunch-time and there she is dealing with one of her little tell-tales. She's so cool the way she does it.

'Miss..'

'Hello Gemma, how are we today?'

'Um, alright miss...'

'Good, good, well off you go then, you're missing lunch-break.'

'Only - miss...'

'Still here Gemma? Don't you want to go out?'

'Yes miss...'

'Off you go then, chop chop.'

'But I saw something miss.'

'Did you Gemma? You must tell us all in circle time.'

'Miss - a boy...'

'A BOY Gemma! You saw a boy - yes, there are boys everywhere in this school aren't there? Out you go now, miss has some papers to sort out.'

'He threw...'

'Threw what?'

'Chewing gum...'

'Goodness Gemma, what flavour?'

'Dunno miss. Spearmint I think. At a bird.'

'Oh dear, did he hit it?'

'It flew away miss.'

'Probably preferred Regular then, off you go now...'

... I so want her to be happy, but the thought of her not being there to hug and say good-bye to before going on to high school makes me unbearably sad.

*　　　*　　　*

Thurs 8th Jan.

There's a letter for me, scrawly handwriting, it's obvious who. The Liar never replied to hers by the way, just said, 'Yes, well I hope that's been a lesson to you..' heavily for the class's benefit, pretending she hadn't noticed anything between the lines.

When I open it there's a slip congratulating me on surviving and wishing me good luck with the book. 'Remember this:' it says, 'you are not the author till it's finished. If you write as the author you'll become a character, who turns up with their dirty washing and won't go. Forget who you are. Forget you even exist until it's done.'

Well that's a peach that is. That's what you get for being friendly, last time I get involved with an author. I chuck it in the bin.

* * *

Friday 9th Jan.

Me, Kim and Heidi, squashed in the stock cupboard in our cloaks and masks, suffocating. We hadn't counted on Hargreaves doing her room first. The Liar ignores him of course, as if he's a piece of dirt himself.

'Can you still hear him?'

'Don't know, shush a minute...'

'What was that?'

'Nothing. Shush.'

'I can still hear him.'

'No, he's gone I think.'

'I'm gonna sneeze.'

'Don't. He might hear.'

'Can't help it. ... Ahh..'

'*Shut* up. He's still there.'

'Just shut up and drive.'

'Eh?'

'Nothing - advert... Shall we risk it now?'

'No. Five minutes minimum.'

'I need the toilet.'

'Tough. If he catches us...'

'I'll wet myself.'

'If it drips on the copying paper you'll be expelled.'

'He is there, listen...'

'What's he doing?'

'Chucking stuff in the bin.'

'Sounds like pencils.'

'Prob'ly is. He chucks away everything off the floor, saw him after netball once.'

'Cheek. I wonder if it was him binned my project.'

'Could have. If it was on the floor he would.'

'Hairy bottom - he should get the sack for that, it's wrong to chuck people's stuff out.'

'Huh, wrong, we can talk - look at us... Shh, he's going...'

'Bout time, I'm busting.'

'Right - fire door, run straight for it. Ready?'

' 'Kay.'

'One.. two.. THREE...'

YeeeeONG... We blitz her good and get the hell out of there. She practically falls off her chair with shock. Ha - they suspended me, I've served my time, but as you wouldn't face your punishment you get to stay right here with us till we're done with you.

* * *

Monday January the 12th.

They took me out of class and told me.

They gave me tea in the office, forgot the sugar, till I was fetched. It wasn't mum, she was back at home having a pow-wow with dad and Uncle Don, sorting things out.

'I'm going to go the long way round,' he said very quietly, starting up, 'past the hospital. If you want to stop, tell me, otherwise we'll just...'

We drove without a word. I let the hospital go past, but he spotted me looking back.

'Come on,' he said.

* * *

I sat in the passage while he had a word with them. They brought tea, I said no but took it. Sweet. He took my cup when I finished. 'This is between you and your grandad.' He put it underneath. 'I'm here, but not here. Take all the time you need, and tell me if you need me. Otherwise, forget I exist.' He squeezed my shoulder, first time, and took the cups.

As I sat there alone a staff door opened and a snatch of music flew out. 'Cause you are beautiful, no matter what they say - words can't bring you down..' Christina. Her voice was so beautiful and clear and the sudden image of Emma and her Cher wig from when he was alive, I had to join in even though it was the completely wrong time and the moment my mouth opened this terrible wailing cry began and went on all through the song which I couldn't hear any more but was singing and mouthing at the same time as if I could right through to the very end.

There was silence in the corridor and clatter from further down. I sat till I stopped feeling stupid and my head cleared. I had to be no-one for him, I couldn't go in as the brave grieving grandchild. Not as a character.

For ages I stayed emptying myself. Here but not here - forget I exist. Till the noises got fainter and joined up. Then I stood and went in.

He lay still, mouth slightly open, not at peace, not at war. Just dead, like a clock that has stopped. Only can never be rewound. I held his hand. Cold, not surprisingly, just dead cold. As I did so one of his silly war stories came back.

'Poppy Harvatt has a soldier in her handbag and skips down the road to the grocer's store thinking of him. She has threepence to buy carrots, sugar and flour to make a cake to send to him at the front. She will bake it slowly and maybe add an eggcup of sherry so it will travel well and keep if held up by the eager columns of soldiers marching down French roads to fight.

He will open it and share it with his pals at a rough table where they read maps and clean their boots after a skirmish. They will share jokes with their mouths full and finish their mugs of tea.

Edward, her soldier, has his mouth open ready to bite, ready to take a bite of the moist rich cake, but it remains open. It will never close. He has died from the last shelling and lies in no man's land where it's too dangerous to collect the bodies.'

Dear sweet gramps. You didn't scare me then and you don't scare me now. I just wanted you to live for ever, that's all. For ever.

* * *

Graham drove me back, not a concerned father figure, just drove. Well, not quite, he was in dad's Beetle, on account of his getting clamped by mistake at the station car-park. We were minus the door my side and a front wing, and back-firing quite frequently and loudly. There were pedestrian lights by Woolworths, we stopped for shoppers to cross. A man, quite young, sat against the window. He had a piccolo but had given up playing. Flurries of legs passed him. Graham had a KitKat on the dash, I nipped out and handed it to him, quite easy without a door. He didn't speak but looked in a puzzled way. He wasn't expecting a young person to do something like that. He tussled it out of the wrapper and gave it to his dog.

In the house, mum, dad and Uncle Don together round the table with long faces, papers and tea cups spread all over. Mum and dad hold arms out for me, someone to hug. Graham stands back till the comforting's over. He puts the Beetle keys down respectfully in front of dad and says very quietly, 'Time to take her now...'

* * *

I forget I am part of life and think only of death. The way it visits. I think of autumn, the woods where we walk through layers of dead leaves, beech-nuts and wettened, rotting bits of branch with fungi.

It is beautiful. The mists and rains damp everything and make it solemn, like a church. The brown of dead branches glistens and goes black, spectacular toadstools take hold where the inside part shows, the meaty woody part. The dying branch nourishes them. Hidden around are paler, smaller ones with subtle shapes and colours - off-whites, greys, russets and browns, they are speckled and flecked lightly, delicately. Sun would shrivel them, they belong in gloom, they are part of it, secretive and silent.

Death gives way to life. We live on the thin layer of richness provided by death, if it gets spoiled life can't go on.

So death must be a stage. You have to take turns, you take your turn in life, you take your turn in death. Death is alive with other forms, bacteria, bugs, mould, fungus. Everything has its job.

I wonder if your turn in life comes round again, that's the only thing. Maybe by helping to nourish some other life you become part of its spirit. The spirit of life. For life to go on things have to rot down and keep going round. I think I like this better than heaven and hell, getting fuller and fuller of people all trying to reunite with loved ones who got there before, or burning but never burnt.

What if you were to, not become some kind of compost for plants, then animals, then humans of a future generation: what if you became a sediment carried to sea by a river, which eventually becomes a layer of the earth's crust and then after possibly a sleep of a couple of billion years emerges as the grain of a piece of granite, or a diamond.

My head spins and I have to stop.

* * *

Saturday 31st of January.

Corrie and Dave. A simple lovely winter wedding, no bridesmaids or palaver, just them.

Me and Kim like always, and Heidi, she's done good,

made it right to the inner circle in record time. I'm really glad for her.

'Oy Kaz.'

'What d'ya want?'

'Can't tell.'

'Why not?'

'Get in trouble. Shh, here comes the bride.'

'Doesn't she look gorgeous.'

'Yeh - didn't look gorgeous last night though.'

'What d'ya mean?'

'Drunk as a fish.'

'Wow.'

'That's not all... Don't tell anyone - she kissed a stripper, and I mean, kissed.'

'A who?' Heidi still lags behind occasionally, but we'll get her right.

'Stripper, North Sea kipper - you know, Full Monty, nudie bloke doing a show.'

'Wow - d'you think they'll get divorced when her fiance finds out?'

'Who, Dave? Nah, not yet anyway.'

'Why?'

'Haven't got married yet. Shh - let's listen.'

They do the vows and when they kiss first there is clapping and as it lasts quite a long time some of the blokes on Dave's side of the church start cheering and whistling. It's like an instalment of Tricia.

While they're doing the register we fill Heidi in about Dave being a rugby player at weekends and coming home drunk after matches, but Corrie not being the type to stay in for him and how she has always sailed close to the wind with fellas. What music she likes, and what a good dancer, and the only worry she has got in life is Dave lost his job recently and hasn't got another one yet.

As you can imagine Heidi is well impressed, which is nice cause it's like one for us commoners. And as you can also imagine, for once Kim's not exaggerating in fact if anything the opposite - Corrie really did kiss the stripper. It was a long kiss apparently, extremely long, and all her mates at the hen-night chanted 'more, more, more, more' and clapped their hands while she was doing it.

The stripper would be quite used to girls grabbing him like that, especially on ladies' hen-nights - but, when Corrie kissed him he stayed kissed. He knew she was about to get married but he slyly went up to one of her friends and gave her his phone number to pass on.

She should have chucked it really, but she didn't cause of the drink.

* * *

After, we went to a hotel for the reception. It was a big do and the hotel was posh. Dave's people had to come miles so they were staying over, so we were all staying over too. A sort of bonding ritual with the new in-laws if that's the word for getting so legless you can't drive back. Even Heidi's mum had given her a pass-out, the three of us in one room and Shaun and Ry next door with Aunt Della's two youngest boys who we hardly ever see. It was obvious they would get on fine after the first fart joke. There were lifts and porters with red jackets and gold buttons to carry cases. The reception was in a big function room. You went in the main lobby and there was a little easel with a black peg-board and white letters fitted into holes, saying, *'WILSHAW PARTY THIS WAY'*. Corrie Wilshaw. Strange. Like a car's ownership papers being changed, don't really know if I want that to happen to me.

There was a lot of champagne and speeches. There were older cousins we also didn't see much of normally, at university and so on. My image of them is the kind of outriders for the whole family, going on ahead looking for prosperity. The only time they seem to get mentioned is if one gets a First in law and that sort of stuff. We were supposed to all be together at one massive round table, but they soon slunk off to talk about uni stuff, mostly drinking and fast sex by the sound of it, so then some of the cousins from Dave's side were the oldest. When the adults chinked glasses and shouted 'To the bride and groom' and 'Cheers' Shaun and Ry and their new side-kicks pretended they had glasses and did pretend cheers as well - first quiet sensible cheers, then loud silly cheers. The two other boys fell in a heap, giggling. They were drunk. Drunk on the atmosphere, not on champagne, drunk on not being watched, and getting away with things.

In one of the speeches there was a joke about leaving their honeymoon flight tickets behind and spending their first night on the runway at Heathrow. Dave made Corrie check, it was all part of the joke for her to have to empty her bag in front of us cause she has a reputation for keeping the kitchen sink in it. She found them and waved them in the air to show everyone, then shoved them together and stuffed them back in any old how. There were some scraps and bits of confetti. Dave scooped them for the bin.

'Hang on, let me check.' It was still out loud, for everyone's amusement.

They both noticed it together: 'THE MIGHTY UNDRESSERS: ADULT SHOW - YOU WILL NOT BE DISAPPOINTED!' Dave smiled and read it out loud. He knew where she had been with the girls and didn't mind. 'Won't be needing that again now you've got me,' he said in a sexy way. Everyone cheered. 'Writing on the back!' someone shouted, clever, as he flicked it on the table. He picked it up again and noticed the number written in biro.

'What's this then?'

Corrie blushed, remembering.

'Phone number on the back of a stripper's card? What's going on?'

Corrie was stumped. She's good at arguments, but not in front of a room full of suddenly totally silent people at her wedding reception.

'O.K. then,' Dave said angrily.. He snatched his mobile and rang the number. We listened, gobsmacked. People wanted to stop it but were paralysed. They had to know too.

Corrie clamped her hand over her mouth and listened.

'... Who are you?'

'...'

'Listen mate, you gave your phone number to my missus. I'll break both your legs.'

'...'

'I don't care what you thought - you need a friggin good slapping.'

'... ....'

He started to wander round with the mobile, deep in conversation. Still no-one moved.

He came back. The call was over. Before she could say sorry, he spoke.

'Guess what babe... I've got a job. Evenings. Good pay - and lots of extras...' He raised his eyebrows.

'Oh no!' Corrie scrunched her face up. 'I don't believe it...'

There was an eruption of laughter, of relieved hysterical laughter and applause. It went on for a long time. Put your money on Corrie and Dave, they'll never let you down.

* * *

She got to the last fifty of Big Brother, by the way. The producers said they'd noticed how confident and talented she was, but they weren't game to pick someone who was about to get married, that wasn't what they were looking for, so she was eliminated near the end.

All I can say is, it's their loss. She would have been brilliant.

Oh, and Michael Duggan did knock over the frankincense tin and it made a loud noise, but that didn't put Heidi off, she just sailed right on as if nothing had happened. The teacher who was doing it comforted Michael and said not to worry, anyone can have an accident, and he felt a right plonker.

* * *

The speeches stopped, but the talk got louder. People crammed at the bar and bought trays of drinks. They paid with twenty pound notes. They were finished with the champagne now - it was all beer, lager, white wine, gin and tonic. There were glasses everywhere, the staff were too busy to clear them.

One of Dave's cousins picked a half empty glass of champagne up from a table where the adults had gone over to the dance floor, and went 'Cheers!', slopping some, and drank it. He looked up with a silly expression pretending to be drunk, only you can't get drunk that quickly, everyone knows. He made his legs go wobbly. We all giggled, cause it was a special entertainment made up just by us. When he giggled, some of the drink came back up and dribbled on the floor. No adult came over, and no-one told us off.

The older ones got more daring - they got another four glasses, all with a bit of champagne in, one nearly full. It wasn't really our entertainment now, there were two separate groups - Dave's cousins had decided to do the routines and our bit was to be the audience and encourage them. They did cheers again. No-one came to stop them. We all giggled and looked at Matt, who had the fullest. He was fifteen so he was the leader. He knew we were waiting for him to see what next, so he couldn't disappoint us.

He went off with another cousin, Bobby - they knew each other properly cause they lived close - and they got a tray and went round the tables. They came back with more glasses, some with champagne, some with other drink. One of the adults had given them money for being so sensible, collecting them.

They did several rounds of cheers, then started doing stupid dances and making fun of the adults who couldn't dance properly or talked in funny voices. Bobby's eyes went wrong and he stumbled. He grabbed for a table as he fell but only got the cloth. It slid off in his hand as he went down and the glasses smashed around him. That stopped the adults.

After the scene-of-crime investigation and big blame session we were split up. Bobby was sitting miserably next to his mum, glancing and wishing.

It wasn't so good now we couldn't muck about. The three of us slid away from the boys, back along the bumpy wallpaper and out. There was another door, it swung back; we went over and pushed through, letting it clack behind. No-one looked, being as we were girls. It was a long corridor, but not the one with stairs up to our room.

There were signs. Male changing. Female changing. Multi gym. Jacuzzi. Pool.

Wow. No-one said about swimming, we hadn't brought cossies. We followed the signs. You went round a corner at the end and just as you thought you were running out of hotel there it was, built onto the back. We looked round and pushed the door. Locked. Through the glass you could see it flat and glistening, just moving enough for the light reflections to be alive and make snakes and ropes, and for the black lane-lines to break and mend themselves endlessly.

There were footsteps and a chink of keys and money. We froze, even though we were guests and doing nothing wrong. There are always rules you don't know about. If we ran now it would have to be towards the fire escape, there was nowhere else, so we stood and waited, alert.

Uncle Don. He emerged round the corner looking lost. It was good to see someone else lost, made him feel found again, so he started taking charge.

'Looking for the toilet then? Me too. None down here though, we've gone too far.'

He looked at the pool for a minute. Uncle Don. Always being the clown, especially at occasions. Though for this one he's been ordered by Corrie to keep it low key. He knew she meant it too, only made four dirty jokes in his whole speech. He thinks he has a way with kids, but he's getting old now - they'd respect him if he'd just sit and be funny sometimes, but he has to dance to Chemical Brothers and spoil it.

'I know what you were thinking...' He looked down knowingly. 'You were going to sneak in for a little dip and do one in the water. Naughty...'

Kim still couldn't stop herself giggling like he wanted her to, it was weird, like she had suddenly gone younger, and he held her hand as we turned back towards the reception room.

Back along the corridor we came to the loos, next to each other.

'Last one out's a pineapple,' he said, and dashed in. We walked on down. Kim tried to explain him to Heidi without sounding apologetic, sad really, your own dad. 'He doesn't know ages, that's the thing. He's O.K. with five-year-olds, he really makes them laugh...'

Back in the party room people are starting to go. The bride and groom have stopped dancing and positioned themselves by the door to shake hands, though they're staying, they're off to Cuba in the morning. It's been a memorable night, someone shouts. The staff are cleaning tables, and the buffet's gone. It's like the end of fireworks night, just empties left.

* * *

Still Saturday (just about)

Bedtime. A real English hotel with soft beds and lavender soap. First time ever, except abroad and that's different.

We pressed the remote and did the channels. Channel Five, wow. But boring. We flicked the others. *'Sex and the City'*. We watched, first time, no adults to make us switch off. It finished. Big deal. Sure they were naked in bits, but not that naked, only the same as a shower ad. Adults have no idea what kids see and do, they really think they're in control.

In bed we lay there, going over the evening. The boys were so funny, with the champagne. And the pool. If only Uncle Don hadn't come, maybe we'd have found a door.

It was dead quiet now, the whole hotel seemed asleep. We lay there listening, tired from the dancing and silly things with the cousins, but wide awake with excitement. Gradually the chat got slower and the other two closed their eyes and dozed off. Maybe if I put the tele on really quiet they wouldn't hear. Adult films, boring, and a chat show. It was too quiet to hear properly anyway.

In the morning we would go after breakfast and wouldn't have had a swim. An idea came. I chucked a jumper and jeans on and in bare feet slipped out of the room leaving the door just touching but not shut. I skipped and tip-toed down the soft carpet of the corridor, like a ballerina. It was easy to follow the fire exit signs and find the pool. But I was right first time - all locked. I pressed against the window. Water always moves, it kind of breathes, and the ceiling lights become snakes. There were only some little ones on, it was just light enough to see, kind of orangey. My eyes started at one corner and drifted along to the other one, searching for doors. There was a small blue one by the changing rooms - worth a try.

I crept round. FILTRATION UNIT. STAFF ONLY No handle, just a lock. I pushed it. Just a minute... It was stiff but you could sense they hadn't locked it. It opened into a dark concrete room with humming.

It was warm. I stood, letting my eyes adjust. There were tiny red lights in places, they didn't light anything up but gradually the edges of things showed themselves, then parts of them - vents and pipework. I tried to focus on the wall at the other side, but it was just dark. Sometimes I thought I saw the shape of a sign or notice fixed to it, then it would go pitch black again. There was no line of light near the bottom that could be a door but I walked carefully over anyway doing pigeon steps and keeping my hands in front, for obstacles. My breath went shallow, almost panting. Middle of the night, dark, in somewhere forbidden and maybe dangerous.

My hands felt the wall at last, rough, concrete. I felt along. A smooth square bit - notice probably, like I thought. I kept on till I got to the corner, and stopped. My eyes getting used to the dark now, I could see shapes: not the wall, but the sign further down - I guessed it was yellow with black writing. DANGER... something or other. I felt my way back, quicker this time, just feeling the wall with one hand and walking forwards, instead of both, going slowly sideways.

I looked straight in front of me. All dark, but at the end where the wall went back along the side to where I came in, a change in the density. Black black and grey black. In a long square that would be about right for a door. I stopped feeling the wall and made my way towards it. Wooden slats, crossways in a kind of window frame. Down the side now - no handle, just a panel to push. Closed.

I strained my eyes and felt again. It was there. Handle - a knob one like on an ordinary door. And with a squeak, it opens, into another dark area, but different noises - trickling water instead of droning. Under my feet the floor changes from smooth to ridged. I'm in a changing room. I feel along again. Pegs for clothes. Hand over hand along to an entrance, through, following the wall still. It's smooth, cold and clammy, feels like the shower part. Must be the pool soon, I can sense it.

Then I can sense something else dangerdanger I can hear breath, agitated, panting. Nothing spoken. I can't figure out where.

A huge hand clamps my mouth from behind, adult hand, strong.

Sweaty. I'm wriggling but no good, clammy sweaty hand, drinkey smokey breath oh God they murder people and do things... Do things first. Your parents on tele crying, begging.

My wriggling slows down, he's too strong, miles too strong, dragging me poolwards; it's time to give in and cry. Police lady, sad-faced, standing next to mum as she begs them to give her daughter back.

But no good.

Then the dim lights and faint slop of water, I was close after all. The hand loosens its sweaty grip, and I'm being scrutinised as a fisherman checks his nets before the gutting.

'HAH - caught you in the act. Bad idea, swimming in the dark, no adults. See what could have happened? I could have been a... a dirty old man. Then what?'

Uncle Don, drunk - swaying with drink - moving his horrid puffy face close to mine as he says the words, pretending he's scaring me to be helpful.

I wet myself as I stood there, not just a bit: my whole body seemed to go slack as if the bones had gone, and I flooded myself.

'Just thinking about a sneaky dip myself. Couldn't find the damn lights though. Good job I...'

He went to put a hand on my shoulder, tenderly, but I ducked away, and in the half-dark tried to wriggle past back to where I thought the utility door was. He wanted to stop me, fat arm flapping like a tentacle.

'I didn't mean to... I hope you don't think..' Hushed voice echoing. More scary. I panicked, pushing past, shoving hard at him. Blindly I ran. There was a huge splash. He was in. I didn't even turn round, he could get himself out horrible pig. I'll tear his birthday cards up for ever and not even keep the money. My knee hammered against the corner of a wall where I thought the door would be. I shoved the pain away to have later. My hands found a wall and slapped along it till it gave way.

There was a blinding light and a shriek. Series of shrieks and howls. Then the first splash. The room I was in lit too, and there it was, just four walls and a boiler thing like at school. Me thinking I was the fearless agent behind enemy lines blah blah..

There were splashes galore now and yowls of laughter. I ran back through the shower place and there they all were - Corrie, Dave, best man, half a dozen of them, all in in their clothes even shoes. Uncle Don sloshing across to join them, to disguise himself as one of them.

'Kazzie! Babe... Come on!'

My bomber did the first two lanes and I was with them, all drunk as fish. Dave grabbed me and flung me across. One of his brothers flung me back. It was a game, I was the beach-ball.

I knew it would get to Uncle Don. When it did I kept up the game. Before he had me right to throw back I flung my arms round his neck affectionately, tight, to block his face from the others, then clamped his head in my hands, thumbs pressing as hard as I could into his eyeballs till I could feel them squash. I kept pressing, I wanted to pop them, then forced him under and held him there.

He couldn't break my grip straight away, and when he came up they cheered cause he'd been dunked by a kid. His hands stayed over his eyes, no-one bothered they thought it was the chlorine. He went quiet and slunk off not long after.

Dave hauled himself out, suit glossy like a seal. On the side they had more champagne, he popped one - the cork shot out and glided gracefully down to the deep end and floated there in its own water like a small seabird. Dave upended the bottle till the foam hit his face, then sprayed it over and over us. Team Wilshaw, winners' podium. The spray died down. He chucked the bottle for Corrie to drink, she was a winner too. She passed it on. We were all winners. When it came to me I tipped it up and drank to the dregs. To me. To everyone. To life. To life, the universe and everything. They cheered and clapped and congratulated Corrie for bringing me up right.

She held out for the empty. When it came over she did a one two three and flung it high over her head like the bouquet. It plopped down by its offspring and they floated peacefully in the deep end together.

* * *

21 of July about

Kazzie's in love. Bit young to be in love at eleven, but she is. She keeps glazing over in lessons. She writes his name in the margins and on tables, she'll get in trouble.

'Is soap powder so important to you you have to write it over the cover of your book?' MacAlly-Pally said to her the other day, feeling pleased with her wit. The kids thought she was pathetic. Daz - God.

Daz is Danny. There isn't a Danny in her class but there's one in year seven in high school, Laura Hill's brother. He got the job of showing her group round on in-thingy day when they go to check the place out. Duction. He's probably OK-looking for a year-seven. Some of the other girls thought it must be him, they got jealous till they realised.

'You can stay in after school and do two sides on the joys of the family wash, if you still find it funny,' Ally-Pally told her. Bit mean, we break up for the summer in three days, then she'll be in seniors.

Kazzie's class collapsed, so she roared at them all, flummaxed. Poor moo, she hates it when us kids grow up and leave her behind. Hope we don't get her back for a second dose now Miss Stany's leaving. We'll be ready this time if we do mind.

That's where she is now, Kaz, detention so I thought I'd do another chapter being as she's left it before the end. It's crap anyway if you ask me, all that apples and pear stuff.

He's all Kaz can think about, Danny, mind he is cool, he eats food with his fingers, he laughs at things, and makes ace faces. He can manage a fair spit too, or dribble anyway.

Our brother.

*　　　　*　　　　*

He has little pink fingers that clutch things. They're tiny. I sometimes get his ball with the bell in and shake it. When Kaz does it he chuckles. When I do it he blinks as if he's frightened.

'You're too close to his face,' mum says, 'do it gently, like this...' She takes it to show me and forgets to give it back.

Sometimes I put my finger out for him to clutch, he likes clutching things, like a baby monkey. Mum says, 'You've got dirty hands, he'll get germs.'

Then he got croup. His face was always red and he coughed tiny coughs like a kitten would do. He wouldn't take his bottle.

He started crying and screaming. Mum was really anxious. It took ages to phone the doctor, she couldn't get through. 'Putting you on hold...' the recorded voice said. 'But my baby...' mum said, but the voice had gone, it wasn't a real one anyway with a person on the end, then there was soothing music. Mum couldn't be soothed though, all she could hear was his cries. I could see the little muscles in his tummy going hard each time.

In the kitchen was his bottle. It was still warm in the pan where mum had stood it. I got sugar, strawberry jam and chocolate sprinkles out the cupboard, mixed them in and took it through, but just as he was ready to drink it, mum came back in.

'STOP!' she shouts at the top of her voice. 'Do you want to kill him?'

In the silence she says in a quieter voice, 'Go up to your room now...'

I was only trying to help. I still had the bottle, so when I got up I tipped it and sucked. Wasn't too bad.

Can't be bothered with this
any more, *I'm going down the park*

THE END

ABOUT PETER HAYDEN

Peter Hayden is the author of the 'Stringy Simon' series, 'The Headmaster's Daughter', 'And Smith Must Score...', and other books (list at the back).

He grew up in Hove and has four sisters – Susan, Rosie, Vinny and Jill - and has also lived in Norway, the Isle of Man and Australia. He is married with three children (Ben, Mike and Carrie) and their house is right by the Severn Valley Steam Railway station in Bewdley, Worcs.

He has visited hundreds of schools in the U.K. doing talks, readings and writing workshops. Details are available on 01299 403 201.

Hobbies as a kid: football, drawing, playing up, collecting cigarette cards, chemistry set, reading sisters' diaries, scrumping.

Hobbies now: football, learning German, balti-cooking, trying to talk cool, tennis, reading, taking the mick.

Team: The Seagulls (Brighton and Hove Albion) – but also ran the Kidderminster Harriers fanzine for a couple of seasons, it was called 'The Keeper Looks Like Elvis'.

Other publications available from

Crazy Horse Press

no postage, order form overleaf:

The Headmaster's Daughter

'I really enjoyed reading it. It was like listening in on girls' cloakroom gossip.' (Berlie Doherty)

'It's the kind of book that you would be sort of drifting with when you start reading it but when you'd finished you'd read it again because you realise how it fits together and appreciate the detail given at the beginning.' (Teenage reader - original available)

Older teens, £5.99 ISBN 1 871870 09 7

The Day Trip

'Lost and late, they board the wrong boat home, merge with another school, and end up on the wrong side of the Watford Gap. Ah - but Mike and Lee have declared their love; and what a day they've all had.' (The Guardian)

Early teens, £4.99 ISBN 1 903285 67 4

The Poppy Factory Takeover: Teenage Writing

Creative writing in the classroom - observations and examples from three decades of writing with children. Includes two humorous verse stories written by teenagers and illustrated by Clinton Banbury.

'There is about the whole book a trustworthiness which carries it all... I hope it gets reviewed at length in the right places.'

(David Hart Birmingham Poet Laureate)

Adult & older teen, £6.99 ISBN 1 871870 12 7

And Smith Must Score...

'I recommend it to anyone looking for a good footy read.' (Nick Hornby)

'A wonderful, charming and witty dose of escapist fiction.'
(Derby Co. F.C. fanzine)

'A football supporter's dream of a book.' (Middlesbrough F.C. fanzine)

Adult & older teen, £6.99 ISBN 1 871870 08 9

ORDER FORM - no postage to pay...

Cut out/photocopy and send to:
Crazy Horse Press
53 Stourport Road, Bewdley DY12 1BH

Please send me the following books by return - all £3.99 with this form:

.... copies of 'Portly Paul Buys a Bed' @ £4.99	= £..............
.... copies of 'Patsy's Parlour' @ £4.99	= £..............
.... copies of 'Stewart and the Alien' @ £4.99	= £..............
.... copies of 'The Conker Champ' @ £4.99	= £..............
.... copies of 'Stewart and the Forest Creature' @ £4.99	= £..............
.... copies of 'The Swiss Army Knife' @ £4.99	= £..............
.... copies of 'The Day Trip' @ £4.99	= £..............
.... copies of 'Sorting the Apples & Pears' @ £4.99	= £..............
.... copies of 'The Headmaster's Daughter' @ £5.99	= £..............
.... copies of 'And Smith Must Score...' @ £6.99	= £..............
.... copies of 'The Poppy Factory Takeover' @ £6.99	= £..............
TOTAL	= £..............

NAME ....

ADDRESS..

....

POSTCODE ....   PHONE ....

I enclose a cheque to Crazy Horse Press for £ ....

Signed: ....